When the Stars Fall

When the Stars Fall

Alexis Harris

Map Illustrated by Kirsten Stiles

RESOURCE *Publications* · Eugene, Oregon

WHEN THE STARS FALL

Resource Publications
An Imprint of Wipf and Stock Publishers
199 W. 8th Ave., Suite 3
Eugene, OR 97401

www.wipfandstock.com

PAPERBACK ISBN: 978-1-6667-0018-3
HARDCOVER ISBN: 978-1-6667-0019-0
EBOOK ISBN: 978-1-6667-0020-6

07/01/21

Dedicated to my family, especially my mom and sister, who listened to me read even when it got annoying. Thank you! Robbin Harris and Morgan Harris

Contents

Prince Aurano

1

Queen Celestia paced nervously back and forth, her flowing blue gown trailing behind her. "I don't know, Garrita," she said, "What if none of the kids show?"

Celestia was a pale beauty, with long, white-blonde hair and blue eyes. Upon her head sat a silver tiara, and upon her face, a worried expression.

"Well, of course, they'll show, milady," Garrita said. She was the lady-in-waiting to the queen, close in age, with brown hair and brown eyes. She sighed, "No matter your station in life, motherhood is the same—full of worrying." She smiled, "Prince Aurano has many friends amongst the neighboring kingdoms. They'll all be thrilled to celebrate his birthday with him. You'll see."

The queen nodded uncertainly.

"Come on," Garrita said, "We must get you to the party."

The two of them headed down the stone corridor of the castle, and to the huge throne room where the party was to be held. It was full of people already, including plenty of young children. Queen Celestia noticed elves, dwarves, and humans alike were present. She was pleased that she had been able to facilitate such relations with non-humans, unlike her predecessors.

"There you are," King Bridgot said, meeting up with his wife. He wore blue royal robes and a silver crown. A cape fell around his shoulders. He had tan skin, curly brown hair, a brown beard—trimmed short—and soft, gray eyes.

She had always loved those eyes. She smiled, "I was nervous for today, but I see we have a great turn-out."

"They're all here for our son," he said, returning her smile.

They headed over to their thrones to await the announcement of their son.

It wasn't long before the announcer said, "Presenting the birthday boy, Prince Aurano of Ivétoiless!"

Everyone applauded as the young prince made his grand entrance. He had pale skin, curly blonde hair, and blue eyes. He wore blue royal robes and a small, silver crown upon his head. As he made his way to the thrones, King Bridgot and Queen Celestia strode forward to meet him.

"Aurano," Celestia said, hugging him, "I can't believe you're eight years old today."

"I know, mom," he said, "Can I go play now?"

"Aurano," Bridgot warned, eyeing him meaningfully, "Be nice to your mother."

"We have to be polite and greet everyone first," Celestia said, "*Then* you can go play with your friends."

Prince Aurano sighed.

"Mommy, mommy!" their daughter yelled, running up. She had wispy brown hair and gray eyes. She wore a little gold dress, with a tiny tiara pinned atop her head.

Queen Celestia scooped her four-year-old into her arms, "What are you doing here, sweetie? You're supposed to be with the nannies during the party."

"I want to play with the kids, too," she said.

"Now, Nastazya," Bridgot said, "You know better than to run off on your own. The kids here are too big for you to play with. Don't worry, at your birthday you'll get to play all night."

"Let's get you back to the nannies," Celestia said, "We don't need you getting lost."

"Princess Nastazya," a familiar voice said.

They turned to see Kgansten the dwarf standing before them. He had a red beard, brown eyes, and ruddy skin. He wore dwarven armor, with a Dwarf Lord medal pinned upon his breastplate.

"Uncle Kgansten!" Princess Nastazya yelled, wriggling out of her mother's arms. She rushed over to give him a hug, dragging her teddy bear behind her.

He wrapped her in a warm embrace, laughing heartily. "Wonderful to see you all," he said.

"Uncle Kgansten," Prince Aurano said, smiling. As his younger sister stepped out of the hug, he took her place, embracing the Dwarf Lord.

"Bridgot, Celestia," Kgansten nodded, acknowledging them respectfully.

"Kgansten," Queen Celestia said warmly, rushing to hug him as well.

Bridgot hugged him after, smiling and patting him on the back.

After a slight pause, Kgansten said, "I don't believe you've met my family." He waved over a pale dwarf woman with flowing black hair and violet eyes, and three identical dwarf children with curly red hair and brown eyes. He wrapped his arm around the woman, saying, "This is my wife, Natasha, and our children, Kganley, Kganzar, and Nedebarth."

"Pleasure to meet you," Queen Celestia said, extending her hand to Natasha.

She shook it, giving her a nod.

"Triplets?" King Bridgot asked.

"Yes, indeed," Kgansten said proudly, "In their terrible twos." He leaned in, adding, "I wasn't sure if I should even bring them, but I wanted you to meet them."

"Hi," Princess Nastazya said excitedly, waving to the three boys.

Nedebarth hid behind his mother shyly, as Kganzar looked to Kganley for assurance. Kganley smiled at Nastazya, nodding to Kganzar. They inched closer.

"You guys wanna play?" she asked.

They nodded, and the four of them ran off, ducking around the party guests, Nedebarth trailing behind.

Queen Celestia summoned a couple of servants to keep an eye on them and turned to Aurano. "I suppose you can go play," she said.

"Yes!" he shouted, taking off and meeting up with his friends, who were terrorizing the food table.

She shook her head. "So, how did you two meet?" she asked, turning back to Kgansten.

"Well," he said, "once I became a Dwarf Lord, hundreds of dwarven women threw themselves at me. I took over the territory of Lord Dingus, and such property and position made me desirable to many of them. Anyway, Natasha came along, and she was a breath of fresh air. She didn't care about any of it. She had status of her own, as a lady of the Dwarven Court. I was able to have a real conversation with her, and she was smart, witty, and charming. She won me over rather quickly." He smiled at her, squeezing her shoulder.

"Yes," Natasha said, "Well, I was used to dwarven men who would acknowledge me for my beauty, and try to romance me. But, Kgansten here barely noticed me. I struck up a conversation with him one day, since I didn't feel pressured by him, and he turned out to be a kind, down-to-earth guy. It didn't take long for us to fall in love."

Bridgot and Celestia smiled at the pair, and then Celestia noticed that King Bridgot's family was waiting to speak with them. "It was a true pleasure meeting you," she said, "But if you'll please excuse us. Enjoy the party. There's plenty of food and drink, and the music will begin shortly."

Kgansten nodded, "Go, do your thing."

They headed over to talk to his family. His mother, Katherine, and his father, George, were there. They were a pair of old farmers with graying brown hair. His father's eyes were brown, and his mother's gray. His older sister, Margaret, was there with her husband, James, and their children: Phillip, Anne Marie, Josephine, Jonathan, and Theresa, ages fourteen, ten, seven, five, and four. It was hard for Celestia to believe how fast they'd grown. The last time they'd been to their village, Phillip was only four, and Anne Marie was a baby.

His brother, Bryan, was there as well, with his wife, Brianne, and their children: Thomas, Bethany, and Sarah, ages nine, six, and three. Thomas had just been born when Bridgot and Celestia got married. Time had really flown since then. She wanted to laugh, thinking of how his brother had always tried to top Bridgot's accomplishments. Yet, here they were. Bridgot was a king, and Bryan was simply going to take over the family farm.

His sister, Kyja, was also present, with her husband, Ethan, and their children: Jada, Karson, and Jewel. Jada was a two-year-old with brown hair and gray eyes, like her mother. Karson and Jewel had blonde hair and brown eyes, like their father. They were twin babies—new additions to the family.

And, lastly, his sister, Luanne, was there with her fiancé, Dillon. Luanne had brown hair and brown eyes, and was quite plump in size. Dillon had red hair and brown eyes, and was rather scrawny. They were an odd match, but she could tell they were happy together, and that's what mattered.

"Wow," Queen Celestia said, "It seems like it's been forever since we've seen you last. You all have grown so much!"

"Yes," Katherine said, "I can't believe we have over a dozen grandkids, now!"

"Congratulations on the engagement, Luanne!" Celestia said, smiling at her and her fiancé.

"Thank you," Luanne said, "We're certainly excited about it."

Dillon smiled, showing the dimples on his freckled face, and putting his arm around her.

"And congratulations to you as well, Kyja," she said, "Can I hold them?"

"Of course," Kyja replied, maneuvering to let Celestia hold her twins.

She gingerly accepted the babies in her arms, looking down at their tiny, sleeping faces. "They're so precious," she said, "I miss the baby days."

"Still hard to believe my little sister's a mom now," King Bridgot said.

Kyja smiled, and they moved forward to hug each other. "How are you?" she asked.

"I'm good, as always," he said, "How have you been?"

"Good," she answered, "The pregnancy was rough this time around, but we made it through."

"I'm amazed you retained your figure," Celestia chimed in, "You look amazing!"

Kyja chuckled, "Thanks."

Bridgot took his turn holding his new niece and nephew, before handing them back to his sister. After a brief session of hugging and catching up, they made their way around the party, greeting all of their guests. As they were getting ready to wrap it up for the day, Celestia heard a familiar voice behind her.

"Sorry I'm late," her mother said, "You know I wouldn't miss my grandson's birthday for the world!"

"Mom!" Queen Celestia exclaimed, turning and embracing her mother.

"Hello, darling," Lady Eva said, "And hello to you as well, Bridgot." She hugged her son-in-law, smiling. Eva had light brown skin, brown eyes, and caramel hair. She wore a flowing, lavender gown and a gold band around her head—a symbol of her previous status as queen. "Where is he?" she asked.

"He's playing with his friends," Celestia said.

"Oh, I suppose I'll wait 'til the party's over to give him his gift, then."

"What'd you get him?" she asked.

"Nothing extravagant," Eva replied.

Celestia shot her mother a suspicious look, "Define 'not extravagant.'"

"It's just a little race track for his wooden cart."

"Mother!" she said, "I told you nothing big!"

"I know, I know," Lady Eva said, "But, he's my grandson. I reserve the right to spoil him."

Queen Celestia sighed, shaking her head.

Just then, a servant burst into the room, looking panicked. He rushed over to them, yelling, "War! War has broken out in the kingdom of Kiteau!"

King Bridgot's eyes widened, and he stepped forward, "What are you talking about?"

"Forgive me, sire," he said, "Kiteau is at war with Chemsson, and they are calling for our aid. What shall we do?"

"How is that possible?" Celestia asked in disbelief, stepping up beside her husband, "The prophecy said there would be a hundred years of peace once we destroyed the dark wizard."

"Send in our troops," Bridgot said with authority, "Ivétoiless will not abandon her allies. Put Karim in charge. I must go to see The Oracle. I leave at dawn."

"Yes, sir," the servant said, rushing from the room.

Everyone began to panic, scrambling to get their children and go.

"Everyone!" King Bridgot shouted, "Relax. Please make your departures in an orderly fashion. The war is not here, but in Kiteau. You are safe to leave."

They all slowed a bit, trying to remain calm, but Celestia could see they were panicked, even still.

"Get the kids," Bridgot said, "It will be up to you to watch over them while I'm gone. I leave the kingdom in your hands."

"Absolutely not," Celestia replied, "If you're going to see The Oracle, I'm going with you."

"Not this time," he said, "The kingdom needs you. Our children need you."

"And I need you," she said, "We're stronger together. Somebody's got to watch your back, to ensure you return."

"Then who will care for the kingdom, and our children?"

"There's only one person I would ask," she replied, "and that's my mother. She has plenty of experience in both categories. She loves both our kids and our kingdom. There's no one better suited for the job, and no one I trust more."

He sighed, "It's too dangerous. What if something happens? If I die, I know you could care for our family and our people in my stead. If we both die, our children are orphans."

"It's a risk we'll have to take," she said, "You know I'm not the type to sit idly by." She paused, swallowing, "My father went into battle alone, and look what happened. I've seen what it's like to raise your children and rule a kingdom on your own. Let me tell you, I couldn't do it. I couldn't live with the knowledge that I might have been able to save you, if only I'd been there."

"I'm coming, too," Kgansten said, walking up, "If there's a quest to be embarked upon, you'll need my help."

Bridgot looked away, sighing once more, "Be ready to set out at dawn."

Once the guests had departed, and they'd set up Kgansten and his family in one of their guest rooms, they went to tuck their kids into bed.

"Goodnight, Nastazya, sweetie," Celestia said, "Be good for grandma. Don't worry, mommy and daddy will be back soon. We love you."

Nastazya nodded as Celestia hugged her tight, giving her and her bear each a goodnight kiss.

Celestia intercepted Bridgot in the hall, as he headed into Nastazya's room, and she headed into Aurano's. He looked perturbed. She entered her son's room, going to his bedside, "Listen, honey, daddy and I have to go somewhere for a few days, okay? We'll be back as soon as we can. We love you guys so much."

"Dad already told me," Aurano said, "He said there's a chance you might not come back." Her son looked away, clutching his blanket to his chest.

"Oh, sweetheart," she said, wrapping him in her arms, "Everything will be okay. Uncle Kgansten's coming with us, and there's nothing the three of us can't do together. Trust me."

He leaned into her hug, and a few tears streamed down his face.

She wiped them away, running her fingers through his hair.

"He told me to look out for Nastazya, and that one day I'll be king, whether you guys train me, or grandma trains me."

"Daddy just likes to be prepared for the worst," Celestia said, "But, trust me, we've done a lot more difficult and dangerous things before, and we're still here. I know we can handle this. We're just going to see The Oracle. That's it. All we're doing is talking. Okay?"

Aurano nodded, running his arm across his face.

"Get some sleep, and be good for grandma while we're gone. Goodnight, sweetie," she gave him a kiss and headed out of his room, closing the door behind her. When she saw Bridgot there waiting, she angrily whispered, "You told him?"

"He needed to know the truth. He's old enough to handle it. He'll have to rule the kingdom one day, with or without us, and as the future king, he has to be prepared for any situation."

"He's eight!" she whispered vehemently, trying not to let their kids hear, "He was in tears when I went in there, worried sick about us! Yes, he's the future king, but that's a burden he shouldn't yet have to bear! You became king with no experience. You should never have told him that."

He looked down.

"Pick a guest room tonight," she said, "because our room is closed." With that, she stormed off down the corridor. Before she got to her room, she stopped in her mother's guest suite, "Mother? Are you up?"

"What is it, darling?" she asked, coming over in her purple nightgown, caramel waves cascading around her shoulders.

"I need to ask you to do something for me," she said.

"Of course, dear, anything."

"Bridgot and I have to go on a quest. We need to see The Oracle, to sort out the matter of this war. I need you to watch over our children, and the kingdom, in our stead."

Her mother was silent for a moment, her face darkening, "You know, I had a conversation like this once before. It didn't end so well."

"I know," she replied softly.

"I won't go through this again," she said, walking over to her bed and sitting down, "I told your father not to go, and he went. He asked me to take care of you and the kingdom in his stead. And, you know what happened? He died. I can't lose you, too. I won't." As she spoke, she crossed her arms, looking away.

Celestia was silent a moment before she said, "Bridgot asked the same thing of me. He wants me to stay behind, and watch the kids and the kingdom while he goes on his own." She paused, venturing into the room, "I have the chance to go with him. I have the chance to watch his back, and to make sure *he* returns. But I need your help. No one else can do the job."

Eva was silent for what seemed like an eternity. "Go," she said finally, "Do what I couldn't. But don't die in the process."

"Thank you, mother!" she exclaimed, hugging her.

She nodded, looking away.

"The kids are in bed. Kgansten's family will be staying here as well, until we return. He's coming with us. Natasha can help you with the kids if you need it. I'll keep in touch through this," Celestia handed her mother a golden mirror.

"What's this?" she asked.

"It's a witch's glass. Witches and wizards can keep in contact with each other through any reflective surface via magic, but keeping in contact with non-magical people isn't possible. We can see them, but they can't see us. So, Merlin invented this device, which allows non-magic beings to communicate with witches and wizards. While I'm gone, I'll be able to talk to you through this."

Lady Eva nodded solemnly, taking the witch's glass from her daughter's hands.

"Thank you," Queen Celestia said, "You don't know what this means to me."

She looked up, "I think I do."

A New Quest

2

When morning came, King Bridgot, Queen Celestia, and Lord Kgansten set out for Abyumo, the land of the wizards and dragon riders, where The Oracle resided. Celestia's brown mare, Razel, was getting old, and so was Bridgot's brown stallion, Samson. She knew this would be their last real outing before they were retired. Kgansten's off-white pony with gray spots, Gjabreel, was still in his prime.

They journeyed through the day, stopping only for lunch. When it grew dark, they stopped to make camp. It had been a long time since they'd journeyed on the road without the royal caravan, and the ground was just as hard and uncomfortable as Celestia remembered. Her royal gown made it worse, its bejeweled bosom and sleeves lying awkwardly against the earth. The blue chiffon of her skirt flowed around her elegantly, but didn't add much comfort against the rigid ground.

"I'll take the first watch," Bridgot said, "You two get some sleep."

It was strange, hearing him say that for the first time in years. Celestia settled in as best she could, trying to drift off. All she could think about was the war, and how the prophecy was wrong, and The Oracle was wrong.

"It's no use," she heard Kgansten say, "Can't sleep." After a pause, he said, "How did you do it?"

"Do what?" Bridgot asked.

"How did you adjust to becoming a father, a husband, and a king? I must admit, I love my wife, but I miss the days of being a dwarven warrior, and our time on the quest of the prophecy. I never thought I'd settle down.

I'm stir crazy! When I heard you say you were leaving to see The Oracle, I just had to jump on the opportunity to get out of there."

"Well, it wasn't easy," Bridgot said, "I can see why she ran away. Royal life really does feel like a prison sometimes. You're not free to do hardly anything. Don't tell Celestia, because I would never want to hurt her, but I'm bored. Being a king, a father, a husband, it's so routine. I miss the days when we were on the road, saving the world from darkness. Even being my village's errand boy was more exciting. I'm suffocating in this life."

"I think we need this quest," Kgansten said, "If for nothing else than to escape our roles for a while, and feel adventure and excitement once more."

Celestia allowed a few tears to roll off her cheeks, soaking into the dirt beneath her. *I had no idea he felt that way,* she thought, *I should never have asked him to be king. Yes, our life has become dull and stagnant, but I didn't realize our marriage had, too . . .*

They journeyed the next day in silence, Celestia pacing herself just a little ahead of the two men, trotting silently. A couple of times, Bridgot tried to catch up and talk to her, but she moved ahead, avoiding him. Finally, he stopped until they found a place to make camp.

"We should reach Abyumo the day after next," Bridgot said as they ate some of the stew they'd packed.

"Yes, we're making great time," Kgansten agreed.

Celestia gave a nod in acknowledgment, but said nothing.

They ate their meal in silence and got situated for the night, Kgansten taking the first watch. The next couple days were long and quiet, as they made their way slowly to Abyumo. By lunchtime the second day, they reached the border, entering the territory of the wizards.

"Queen Celestia," Thaandor called, coming to meet them. He was an old wizard with a long, gray beard, a pointed hat, and a magic staff.

"Thaandor," Celestia said warmly.

"King Bridgot, Lord Kgansten," he said, acknowledging them.

"Thaandor," they said together, nodding in return.

"How's the training coming?" he asked, turning back to Celestia, "We haven't spoken in a while."

"I haven't had much time of late," she replied, "But, I've been practicing the spells we worked on."

"It would be easier for you with a staff or a wand to conduct your powers through."

"I told you, Thaandor," she replied, "I just want to be able to control my powers. I'm not interested in joining the land of the wizards."

"Very well," he said, "What brings you here?"

"We have come to see The Oracle."

He nodded, silently leading them to the home of The Oracle. Thaandor was her guardian—her protector and keeper. The home of The Oracle was a tall, elliptical building, made entirely of ivory. It glowed faintly, due to the light The Oracle gave off.

As they approached, the door opened, releasing a blinding light and gust of wind as Celestia ventured inside. The Oracle was just as she remembered. She had golden and amber hair, which seemed to float around her. Her eyes glowed white, with no pupil or iris. She wore a sheer turquoise ensemble, which covered only the essentials.

"Welcome, Celestia," she said, "It's been a while."

"Indeed," she said.

"Why have you come?"

"I think you know the answer to that," Queen Celestia responded, "Although, you've been wrong before."

"So, you think I was incorrect in my prophecy. Is that it?"

She was silent.

"I told you that you had to stop the ritual of the dark wizard, Nazirdok. You did. Unfortunately, it was not enough. Though you destroyed his body, you did not destroy his powers. Therefore, the ritual was not completely thwarted. His powers linger on, and until they are destroyed, the peace will not last."

Celestia paused, considering, "How do I destroy his powers?"

The Oracle smiled, "They will have gone into one of the ritual objects for their own survival. Once his body was destroyed, they needed to take another form quickly, else be destroyed with him. You must find the object and destroy it. To do so, you will need a weapon from each of the five races: human, wizard, dragon rider, elf, and dwarf. You will also need a warrior from each one to wield them. They each must strike the object in which the powers are concealed, and they will be destroyed."

"How will we know which object it is?" she asked, feeling a knot in her stomach at the prospect of another quest.

"Only you can tell which weapons are needed, and which object his powers are concealed within," she replied, "You'll be able to sense it. Trust your instincts. You're the only one who can guarantee the peace of the land, yet again."

She paused again, looking around the ivory room, "I've always wondered, how is it I was able to defeat him?"

The Oracle smiled again, "Now, that is the right question. Unfortunately, you are not ready to hear the answer. Return at the end of your quest, and I shall tell you what you seek to know. For now, know this: you may fill in for any of the five warriors, as the princess of the prophecy, but only one."

Celestia sighed.

"Send in your warriors. I have a few things to tell them as well."

"No one's going to die this time, are they?" she asked.

The Oracle shook her head, "You can't let fear guide your life. Now, go."

She headed back outside, sending Bridgot and Kgansten in. It felt like déjà vu, and it brought back bad memories.

"I have a gift for you," Thaandor said as they were waiting, "I know you don't desire to live here in the land of the wizards, but you can still use it." He pulled out a beautiful wand, carved from a white birch tree.

She took it, letting it rest in her hands for a moment. "Thank you," she said finally.

He nodded. After a pause, he said, "I shall have to teach you how to use it, though. It helps you conduct and control your powers, but only if you know what you're doing."

She sighed, "I suppose it could only help, as we have another quest to embark upon, potentially more difficult than the last."

"I know," he said.

Celestia looked at him, "What do you mean, you know?"

Thaandor returned her look, "The Oracle told me. It seems you shall need my help this time around."

"She didn't mention that to me."

"She only mentions what she sees fit to tell you," he replied, "I believe she did say you would need a wizard, did she not?"

Celestia looked down at the wand she was holding, "Yes. We need a warrior from each race, and a weapon as well."

"I can help you get a wizard weapon. She said you will know which weapon we need when you see it. I shall take you to The Wizarding

Museum, and once we know which weapon we need, help you petition the wizard council to borrow it."

"Thank you, Thaandor," she said, tucking the wand into her dress.

Just then, Bridgot and Kgansten emerged.

"You all are welcome to stay with me tonight," Thaandor said, "Tomorrow, we shall set out north for The Wizarding Museum."

They followed Thaandor until they reached the base of a mountain. There was a small range on the border of the territory of the wizards. They began hiking up the side, following the old wizard. The air grew thin and foggy before they reached a small hut. Inside, it appeared to expand before their eyes. It was a spacious, rustic cabin, spreading outwards around them. It had a cozy feel to it, and Celestia could sense the presence of magic. The furniture was soft and inviting. Warm colors decorated the walls and furniture, and she could see two long hallways. It was far larger inside than it was out.

"This way to your rooms," Thaandor said. He led them down the right-hand hall, and to two guest rooms, side by side—one for Kgansten, and one for Bridgot and Celestia. They were quaint, each with enough room to sleep comfortably. There was a large bed, two end tables, and a wardrobe in each. They thanked Thaandor for the accommodations and got settled in to sleep.

As Celestia lay in bed, ready to drift off, she lifted the small, handheld mirror from the end table. She pictured her mother clearly in her mind, and gripped the mirror, saying, "*Balgadeer.*"

Lady Eva appeared in the mirror, "Celestia?"

"Yes, mother, it's me," she said, "Good to see the witch's glass works."

"Indeed," she replied, "I wasn't sure how this thing would go. I've been keeping it with me at all times, waiting for your call. It started buzzing, and when I lifted it, there you were."

"It's going to take a bit longer than expected," she said solemnly.

"What do you mean?" Eva asked anxiously.

"We spoke with The Oracle today," she said, "Our previous quest was incomplete. We have to finish it if we are to put an end to this war."

Lady Eva looked away, "How long?"

Celestia was silent a moment, "I'm not sure."

Her mother looked pained as she said, "Do what you must. Keep in touch as you go."

"I will, mother," she answered, "I promise." As Bridgot stirred beside her, she whispered, "Gotta go. Love you." She severed the connection, laying the mirror back on the end table, and drifting off to sleep.

When morning came, they set out with full saddlebags, courtesy of Thaandor. He rode upon his gray, speckled stallion, Chevron, leading the way. As they ventured further into the land of the wizards, Celestia felt the presence of magic grow stronger. The grassy plain felt as ancient as the forest of the elves. Each flower told a story, and she felt connected to everything around her. It gave her a sense of fear and fulfillment at the same time. Suddenly, a phoenix flew past overhead, seemingly in a panic. She had never seen one of these incredible, flaming birds look fearful. Just then, they saw a blinding flash of light and flame. It was followed by a crash that they could both hear and feel, as the earth shook beneath them.

"What was that?" Celestia asked as she tried to calm her horse, smoke filling the air.

"A star fell," Thaandor said, looking as though he'd seen a ghost.

She followed his gaze through the smoke, and saw a large lump of flaming rock at the center of a crater, the edge of which wasn't far from where their horses were standing. They leapt from their steeds, venturing closer—all except Thaandor.

The flames began to die down, and the smoke to clear. The crater was massive, spanning half a mile in every direction. Celestia turned her gaze toward the heavens, and noticed the stars that had aligned during the ritual were still in place, as if they had remained frozen in time, unmoving. She also remembered that there had been seven stars at the end of it all. There were now six.

"Thaandor," she said, heading back to Razel's side, "Did The Oracle mention anything about this to you?"

He seemed frozen in fear for a moment, and then looked at her, nodding.

"What did she say?" she demanded.

Bridgot and Kgansten returned, intrigued, as Thaandor said shakily, "Th-the s-stars that were once aligned will soon fall. The prophecy must be completely fulfilled before the last one falls, else Nazirdok's powers will be released, and the world's events will start over again."

"Start over?" Kgansten asked.

He nodded, "Nazirdok will be reborn, and all the events of the prophecy will be as if they never were. Another princess, born at the turn of *this* century, will then have to stop him, with the same stakes. The original quest will have been for nothing."

The three of them looked at each other, and then back at Thaandor, speechless.

"We must hurry," he said finally, "Time is already starting to run out." He urged his horse forward, as the rest of them scrambled back onto their horses to follow.

When they stopped to make camp that night, Bridgot asked, "So, what are we supposed to be doing, precisely? The Oracle didn't exactly give us a five-star explanation."

As Celestia opened her mouth to answer, Thaandor said, "We must find the ritual object which contains Nazirdok's powers, and destroy it with a weapon and warrior from each of the five races: human, dwarf, elf, wizard, and dragon rider."

"Yes," Celestia said, "That's exactly right. And, apparently, we have a time crunch now." After a pause, she continued, "Well, we have a human warrior—Bridgot, a dwarven warrior—Kgansten, and a wizard warrior—Thaandor. So, we need only two more warriors—dragon rider and elf—and we need all of the weapons."

"We have weapons," Kgansten said, pulling out his axe.

"No," she replied, "We need particular weapons. The ones we have won't work. We have to find the right ones."

"Only she can," Thaandor added, "According to The Oracle, she'll be able to sense the weapons when she's near them. That's why we're headed to The Wizarding Museum—to find the wizard weapon we need."

Everyone sat in silence for a moment, before Bridgot asked, "So, you can find the weapons, but you won't be wielding any of them?"

"I can fill in for any of the warriors, as the princess of the prophecy, but only one. So, we still need at least one of the other races to grant us a warrior. I can only stand in for one of the two."

"Let's get some rest," Thaandor said.

Everyone lied down to sleep as the old wizard took the first watch.

They journeyed the next day, covering as much ground as they could. When they stopped to make camp, Thaandor said, "We should reach the museum tomorrow. It houses a great number of wizard weapons. It's likely the one we need will be there."

"I hope so," Bridgot said, "Because having a timer on this quest puts even more pressure on us to find everything we need quickly."

"Indeed," Thaandor agreed, "We will have to keep moving once we find it. This quest will not be easy, and it will not be quick. We can only hope that it will be quick *enough*."

"I wish Aurano and Nastazya were here," Kgansten said, "Then, we wouldn't have to worry about finding two more warriors, and they could help us get access to the weapons."

Celestia hadn't thought about their fallen friends, namesakes of her children, for a long time. Their mention brought back painful memories that she had since repressed. The great elven and dragon rider warriors who had bravely sacrificed their lives on their first quest would always hold a place in their hearts. She hung her head as she said, "I wish they were here, too."

"As do I," Bridgot said, "But it does no good to dwell on the past. We must focus on the quest ahead of us. Their sacrifice will not be for nothing."

"Aye," Kgansten agreed.

Celestia nodded solemnly. After a pause, she said, "Get some sleep. I'll take the first watch."

Everyone nestled in for the night, and she took her post to watch over her sleeping warriors. Once it seemed everyone had dozed off, she began counting the blades of grass within her field of vision, just trying to pass the time.

"Hey," Bridgot said, coming up and sitting beside her.

She looked away.

"Are you still upset with me for what I said to Aurano?" he asked.

She was silent.

"I'm sorry," he said, "You were right. I shouldn't have said that."

She still didn't answer.

He sighed, "Look, I'm doing my best here. I know I don't always get it right, but I'm trying. I love our son, too."

Celestia turned to face him, allowing her emotion to show on her face. "Is our marriage dying?" she asked.

"What?" he questioned in surprise, "Of course not. Why would you think that?"

"I heard what you said to Kgansten the other night."

His eyes widened as he struggled to find words. After a pause, he said, "I didn't want you to hear that. I'm sorry you did."

"Me, too," she said, rising to walk away.

He grabbed her arm, "Celestia. I love you. I love our family, more than anything in the world. I just never thought royal life would be *this* restrictive. I feel like I understand you more now. I understand why you ran away."

"I'm sorry, too," she said, pulling her arm away, "I'm sorry I asked you to be king. I'm sorry I've made your life so boring and routine that you feel like you're suffocating."

He opened his mouth to say something, but nothing came out.

She let loose a tear as she turned and walked away.

The next day, they reached The Wizarding Museum in the late hours of the morning. It was a huge structure, about the size of the dragon riders' banquet hall. It was made from gray stone, which glistened when the sunlight hit it. It had several massive windows and a pair of towering doors. Celestia could feel the tangible presence of magic all over it.

"Here we are," Thaandor said, "Shall we?" He gestured to the doors, and they all dismounted, tying their horses to the posts outside.

They ventured through the doors, and Celestia marveled at the magnificent and ancient museum. The central area housed a great, golden statue of Merlin, with several paintings done by magic adorning the walls. There were five corridors leading from the center.

"This way to the weapons," Thaandor said, beginning to walk toward the left-most corridor.

"What else is this museum home to?" Celestia asked in wonder.

He paused, "You like it? Yes, it is an incredible place, full of centuries of magical artifacts. Each corridor leads to a different section of the museum. There are shrines to famous wizards, magical animals, magical objects, works of magical art, and much more. The center, of course, is a tribute to Merlin himself—the greatest wizard of all time."

She looked about in awe, wishing they had time to explore the whole place.

As if reading her thoughts, Thaandor said, "Unfortunately, we don't have the time to wander about. Come on."

They followed him down the corridor, past many wands and staffs displayed in glass cases. Each one had a story of the witch or wizard to whom it belonged, posted on a silver plaque beside it.

"Where are the guards?" Bridgot asked.

"It's a *wizard* museum," Thaandor replied, "All of the pieces are protected by magic."

As soon as he'd said it, they heard a shock of electricity and a crash, as Kgansten touched one of the glass cases, and was sent flying backward.

"Don't. Touch," Thaandor emphasized, eyeing Kgansten meaningfully.

"Now you tell me," Kgansten retorted, as he struggled to reach his feet.

Thaandor turned to Celestia, "Do you feel anything yet?"

She tuned in to the environment around her, trying to connect with any of the magical pieces. She felt nothing—nothing out of the ordinary. "No," she answered. After a pause, she said, "What if The Oracle was wrong? How will I be able to tell which weapons are right? What if I don't feel anything?"

"You still doubt The Oracle?" he smiled, shaking his head, "I have worked with her a long time. She has never been wrong. Trust me, when you near the right weapon, you'll feel it."

Celestia twisted her lips doubtfully, as they continued following Thaandor down the long corridor of wizarding weapons. Wand after wand and staff after staff, she felt nothing. Time was not on their side, and the burden of being the one who could find the necessary weapons weighed down on her more and more with each display. As they turned a corner, she felt a twinge. Something was pulling her toward it. Her eyes scanned the room and landed upon a glass case. It was illuminated brightly, and inside there lay a wand. It called to her. Everything around her faded away, and she walked right up to it, feeling the tingling sensation of magic coursing through her.

As she reached out to touch it, Thaandor shouted, "Don't!" But it was too late. She placed her hands on the glass case. He drew nearer, staring at her in amazement, "How did you do that?"

"Do what?" she asked, breaking out of her trance.

"These cases are protected by magic."

"I'll say," Kgansten grumbled.

"How is it you were able to touch the case without being shocked?"

She shook her head, "I don't know. I felt pulled to this case. I think this is it. This is the wizard weapon we need to destroy Nazirdok's powers."

Thaandor drew nearer, peering at the case more closely. He gasped, and then sighed, shaking his head in disbelief.

Celestia shot him a questioning look, "What?" As she waited for a reply, she turned to the silver plaque beside the wand.

"It had to be the wand of Merlin," Thaandor said.

Wizards and Dragon Riders

3

The four of them set up camp outside the museum, as Thaandor pooled a large puddle together in front of them. "I'll need your help for this one," he said, looking at Celestia.

Her eyes widened, and she shook her head as she said, "How would I help? I'm not that good at spells, yet."

"You can do it," he assured her, "It's not that hard." He paused, "You'll need your wand, though."

"Your wand?" Bridgot asked, looking at her.

"Yes," Thaandor said, "I gave her a wand as we were waiting for the two of you at the home of The Oracle." He returned his gaze to Celestia, "Using a wand is easier than using your hands. It's merely a tool, granting you precision and control, when used properly. It's a conductor of sorts for your powers."

She took the wand from the folds of her gown, staring at it.

"Now, to use it, you simply aim it at the target of your spell and focus your energy through it. When you're ready, recite the incantation, and allow your powers to flow through the wand."

She stood there uncertainly, still staring at it.

"We're doing a very simple spell to start," he said, "The first one you ever learned, in fact. You use it all the time. It should be a breeze for you."

"*Balgadeer*," she whispered.

"Yes," he said, "Now, I'll go first. Once I call forth the wizard council, you will need to focus in on them and aim your wand at the image. Recite the spell as normal, and we will be able to share the required energy to sustain the spell."

She nodded, still unsure.

He waved his staff over the puddle, casting the spell, and several old, bearded wizards appeared on its surface, sitting around a table. They seemed to have been waiting for their call.

Celestia focused in on them, using the picture before her, and aimed the wand at the puddle, reciting the incantation. When she did, blue magic streamed from her wand, striking the surface of the water. It caused no ripples, however. It simply spread over the image seamlessly. Once the spell was cast, she could feel it draining her energy, and she could feel Thaandor's powers working with her own.

"Thaandor," they said, nodding.

"Councilmen," he responded, "I have called this meeting to discuss the matter of The Oracle's prophecy."

"We know," the head councilman said, "She told us everything. She said the queen would need to borrow one of our weapons to ensure the success of the prophecy's fulfillment. Only she can know which weapon will be required. I presume you have shown her to the museum, and therefore, know which weapon you need. So, you are calling upon us for permission to borrow it?"

"Yes, councilman," Thaandor replied.

"Well, of course we shall grant it," he said, "Us wizards understand the consequences the failure of this quest entails."

"So," another councilman asked, "Which weapon is it?"

Thaandor and Celestia exchanged glances nervously. Finally, he looked back at the council, "The wand of Merlin."

There was a long pause, during which the councilmen exchanged glances with one another, and looked back at Celestia and Thaandor in disbelief. Finally, one of them said, "'Tis impossible. Any other weapon, of course, but *the wand of Merlin?* The greatest wizard of all time? Our most prized historical artifact? It can't be done."

"He's absolutely right," another chimed in.

"Councilmen," Thaandor said, "I ask you: does it not make sense that the wand needed for such an important and ancient prophecy would be the most powerful wand in existence?"

They were silent again, before the head councilman spoke up, "Due to the importance of this quest, I'm inclined to grant you approval, but, with a time limit. The wand is to be returned to the museum in no more than six months. If it is not returned in time, no spell in the world will be powerful enough to conceal you from the wrath of this council."

After a pause, Thaandor said, "Very well. We accept your terms."

He nodded, "The spell protecting the wand shall be lifted at dawn. Take it from its case with care, and see that it is promptly returned."

With that, Thaandor severed the connection, and the wizard council faded away, leaving only a puddle once more. Celestia felt the same drain she felt when using the spell on her own, and she knew it was due to the length of their conversation. She could see why he had needed to share the load with her.

"We'll be cutting it close with only six months," Bridgot said, "The traveling, plus the time needed to negotiate for the weapons and warriors . . . I'm not sure if that will be enough."

"It'll really take that long?" Celestia asked. She hadn't been sure how long it would be, but she hadn't imagined six months or more.

"Yes," Thaandor agreed, "It will be a challenge. But it's not impossible. We were in no position to negotiate. That was the only way the council would have granted us permission to take the wand of Merlin. I took what we could get."

Bridgot sighed, nodding, "We set out at dawn, then."

As the yellow and orange rays of the sun peeked over the grassy plain, they entered the museum, heading straight for the wand. Celestia lifted the lid of the glass case, taking the long, viney wand, carved from the bark of a willow tree, from within. She carefully handed it to Thaandor, who took it gingerly, staring at it in amazement. It took a moment before he tucked it into his grayish robes, and they headed out of the museum.

"I never thought I would wield the wand of Merlin," Thaandor said as they mounted their horses. He still wore a look of amazement upon his face.

"Not to interrupt such a monumental moment for you," Bridgot said, "But, where are we headed?"

He shook his head, breaking his trance, "The land of the dragon riders," he answered, "We must find a weapon and a warrior from them."

"I hate dragons," Kgansten grumbled as they set out.

They journeyed the next few days through the land of the wizards. They had to go back south near The Oracle, and west into dragon rider territory. The border between the realms was just as magical as Celestia remembered. One minute, they were standing upon the grassy plain of the wizard realm, and the next, they were in the hot desert of the dragon rider realm. She could see the colossal dragon rider city in the distance, with dragons circling in the air. They looked like bats from this distance, and she couldn't yet see the mountains beyond the city.

The four of them crossed the dusty plain, watching as the city grew before them. When they reached the drawbridge, the guards recognized them, granting them access. They entered cautiously, breathing slow. Celestia's eyes widened in fresh amazement at the massive size of the dragons. Some of them were the size of buildings. She remembered when she had ridden upon one, and the terror and elation the experience had brought her.

They ventured through the city and to the glittering, emerald palace. They were welcomed by Loretta, who led them to Kirstiana's throne room. She was the queen of the dragon riders. She had amber eyes and auburn hair, and was garbed in gold. Her amber dragon, Solstra, shared her throne room with her, ever napping by her side.

On seeing them, she rose, looking concerned, "What brings you here?"

"Kirstiana," Thaandor said, opening his arms in greeting, "There is no need to worry. We have come to speak with you, as friends."

She squinted her eyes suspiciously, "About what?"

He sighed, "You've always had a way of seeing right through the intentions of others. There's no point in beating around the bush. Alright, we've come to once again ask you for your help."

She sat back in her throne, observing each of them before she said, "What help do you require *this* time? Do you wish to send another of my dragons and riders to their deaths?"

"Of course not!" Thaandor cried.

"We loved Nastazya, and Ezmyra," Celestia said, stepping forward, "We never wanted them to die."

"They made a choice," Bridgot said, softly but firmly. Thaandor and Celestia stood aside as he continued, "They understood the importance of the quest, and were willing to sacrifice themselves for it. For us." He paused, taking a breath, "If we fail *this* quest, they will have done so for nothing. Everything we went through, everything we did, will have no meaning. If you truly cared for them, you will not allow their memory to be dishonored so irrevocably. You'll help us once more."

Kirstiana sucked in a breath, and Celestia wasn't sure whether she'd swallow her pride or explode. Before she opened her mouth, Solstra stirred beside her, snorting smoke, and looking as though she were speaking to her rider. After a long pause, she turned back to them, saying, "What do you need?"

Celestia breathed a sigh of relief as Thaandor explained the situation to her.

When he was finished, she carefully looked at each of them once more, contemplating her response. Finally, she said, "I will allow you to speak before the dragon rider council. I cannot guarantee their willingness to grant your requests, but you must understand their position. The last time we extended you our aid, it didn't go so well."

They bowed their heads solemnly.

"This way," she said, descending her throne and leading them to the chamber where the council assembled. Celestia recalled the large archways surrounding the room, and their purpose: to allow dragons to stick their heads inside, and join in on the council meetings.

They took their seats beside Kirstiana and awaited the council members' arrival. Loretta had summoned them, and one by one, they arrived, taking their seats around the long, rectangular table. Their dragons stuck their heads inside, waiting patiently to hear what the meeting would hold.

Once they were all seated, Kirstiana began, "Everyone, I have summoned this meeting for sake of the princess of the prophecy. Well, now, queen. She and her warriors once again request our aid." She nodded to Celestia, taking her seat.

Celestia rose, looking around the room at the riders gathered there. The last time she'd spoken before them, she was a princess. She was a girl. She wasn't sure what to say, and she'd been nervous about the concept of dragons. Now, she was a queen. She was a woman. She understood dragons, and she was confident in her message. She met their eyes as she began, "As you all know, the last time we were here, we requested to borrow dragons, in order to reach Khanjgi in time. On that quest, we lost two dear friends: Nastazya and Ezmyra."

The assembled riders bowed their heads upon mention of their names, and she could see their grief over the losses. She felt the same sadness, and she hoped her empathy showed on her face as she continued, "They died to give us the chance to fulfill the prophecy, and complete our quest. Now, war has broken out. It may have started in the land of Duwazo, but it will spread. It will infect all lands. The Oracle told us if we fulfilled the prophecy, the world would know one hundred years of peace. We thought we had been successful, until now."

They looked at her questioningly as she paused, allowing them to process what she was saying, "We have learned that Nazirdok's body was destroyed, but his powers linger. If we do not destroy them, Nastazya and Ezmyra will have given their lives for nothing. The prophecy will be as if it never was. In order to destroy them, we need a warrior and a weapon from each of the five races: human, dwarf, wizard, elf . . . and dragon rider. We come to you today to request both."

The members of the council began whispering amongst each other, looking to their dragons, and processing what she'd said. She took her seat as Kirstiana rose again, "They require a particular weapon that only she can determine. I think we should allow them to figure out which weapon they need, and then make our decision on each of their requests. So, for now, meeting adjourned."

They rose from their seats reluctantly, some looking unsure, some looking understanding, and some looking as though their answer was already *no*. Once they'd departed, Kirstiana looked at them, "Follow me."

She led them through the great dragon rider city, and to their Hall of Weapons. They hadn't yet seen the entirety of the city, as it spanned many miles. Everything was colossal in size, made to provide room enough for their dragons. Dust and dirt flew through the air. There were no plants in the dragon rider realm to anchor the dirt, due to the fiery breath of the great dragons. Their city manufactured weapons for many of the dragon rider cities in their realm, so it was filled with blacksmiths at work. Dragons came and went as they pleased; flying around, starting fires, and circling the distant mountains. The buildings were constructed from stone, with roofs of metal, to avoid them catching fire. All except the palace, of course, which was made from raw emeralds and diamonds, with a floor and roof of gold.

The Hall of Weapons was beautifully constructed of gray stone, its metallic roof shining in the sunlight. As they entered, Celestia marveled at the wide array of dragon rider weapons. They had swords, bows and arrows, crossbows, magic staffs, and even dragon teeth and talons.

She began walking through, peering at each weapon carefully. There were weapons from many famous dragons and riders. Their stories left

Celestia in awe. One, in particular, was about a dragon and rider who went up against a dark wizard. His powers threatened the land, but they were able to overcome him in the final throes of battle. They went down as heroes, preserving their names in the pages of history. The rider's name was Dacron, and his dragon was Vondreer.

It took them the remainder of the afternoon to get through the entire place. After peering at each one, none of them called to her. None of them gave her the feeling she'd had when she'd seen the wand of Merlin.

"How can that be?" Kirstiana asked.

"These aren't *all* of the dragon riders' weapons," Thaandor said, "The weapon we need must be in another location."

Kirstiana sighed, "Perhaps it's in another city. In which case . . . *our* council may not be the ones you need to seek permission from."

"Perhaps," Thaandor said, seeming frustrated, "Are these *all* of your city's weapons?"

"I'm afraid so," she replied, "Other than active riders' own weapons, and . . . " She trailed off, looking back toward the castle.

"What is it?" he asked.

"The shrines," she whispered. After a pause, she turned back toward them, "The only other weapons we have in our city would be upon the shrines of our more recently fallen heroes. You're welcome to look through them when we return to the castle."

Thaandor nodded, "Very well."

They headed back to the palace, and Kirstiana pointed them to the shrines, saying, "I have other matters I must attend to. If you find the weapon you need in there, inform Loretta. I shall call for a council meeting tomorrow, to determine if we shall grant you permission to borrow it. If not, inform her as well, so I can inform the council that it is not we who shall have to grant permission. You all are, of course, welcome to stay here in the meantime. Loretta shall prepare your rooms for you."

"Thank you, Kirstiana," Thaandor said, "We appreciate your help."

She gave him a nod, gliding off down the corridor.

The four of them ventured to the shrines of the fallen dragons and riders. They each had a beautiful painting, a few candles, and a tooth or a talon from the dragon. They walked solemnly through, bowing their heads respectfully.

"Do you think Nastazya and Ezmyra's shrine is still here?" Bridgot whispered.

"Yes," Thaandor said, "I think it is. It will be years before it is moved to the Hall of Weapons."

As they wandered past the shrines, they found it. Seeing the painting of the two of them brought a fresh wave of grief over them. As that hit her, so did another feeling. She felt drawn to their shrine. Queen Celestia allowed a tear to roll down her cheek as she said, "It had to be Ezmyra's talon."

They informed Loretta that they had found the weapon, and then went to their rooms, washing up, and getting situated to sleep. While Celestia was washing up, she gathered a bowl of water, placing it on the sink in the bathroom. She quickly called upon her mother, trying not to take too long, since the others were waiting.

"Hello, my darling," Lady Eva said, "What news?"

"Hello, mother," she answered, "We're in the land of the dragon riders. We're negotiating with them to gain their help with our quest."

"How is that going?"

"I'm not sure yet. We first had to find what we needed from them. We have a meeting with the dragon rider council tomorrow. Hopefully, they'll help us."

Her mother paused, "Why don't you say goodnight to the kids?"

She hesitated, and then nodded, "Very well."

Eva ventured into Aurano's room and woke her grandson. Celestia could hear her talking to him for a minute, telling him his mother wanted to tell him goodnight through a magic mirror. Suddenly, her son's face appeared on the surface of the water, "Mom?"

"Hi, sweetie!" she said, smiling.

"Mom!" he said, gripping the witch's glass.

"How are you doing?"

"I'm fine," he said, "Nastazya misses you guys. When are you coming home?"

"I'm not sure, sweetie," she replied, "It will probably be a few months."

He looked down sadly.

"Hey," she said, "Don't worry. Everything's going well. Daddy and I talked to The Oracle, and she told us what we have to do to stop the war."

Prince Aurano nodded, looking away.

"We're going to make home safe again for you . . . for all of us. I love you, sweetheart. Be good for grandma. I gotta talk to your sister now. I don't have much time."

"I love you, mom," he said.

With that, Eva gave him a kiss, and headed into Princess Nastazya's room, waking her.

"Mommy?" she asked, wiping the sleep from her eyes.

"Yes, angel, I'm here," Celestia said, "How are you? Are you being good for grandma?"

Nastazya nodded eagerly, "Yeah. I got to ride a horse today!"

"Good," she replied, smiling, "My big girl."

"Yeah. Mr. Beary was scared, but I'm not," she said proudly.

Celestia chuckled, "That's wonderful, dear. Listen, mommy's got to go, but I love you."

"I love you, too, mommy!" Nastazya said.

"Goodnight," she said.

"Goodnight, mommy!"

With that, Eva took back the witch's glass, tucking Nastazya in, and heading back into the hallway.

"Well, I've got to go, mom," Celestia said, "But, thanks for letting me talk to them."

"Of course, dear," she replied, "Get some sleep."

Celestia released the connection as she said, "Goodnight."

When morning came, they followed Loretta to the council room, taking their seats beside Kirstiana once more. The rest of the council came in, assembling around the table. Kirstiana rose, clearing her throat, "We all know why we're here. We have come to decide whether to offer our help to the princess of the prophecy once more. They have found the weapon they need, and are ready to make an official request." She turned to Celestia, "Which weapon is it?"

Queen Celestia rose, "The weapon the prophecy requires is . . . " she trailed off, looking from Kirstiana to Thaandor, to Bridgot and Kgansten. Her eyes wandered around the room at the assembled council as she finally said, "The talon of Ezmyra."

Hushed voices and exchanged glances filled the room, before Kirstiana waved her arm to quiet them. After they settled down, she said, "She gave us her argument yesterday. Now, we know which weapon they require. Are there any counter-arguments before we vote?"

A councilman with dark skin rose. Celestia recognized him as the one who'd spoken against them borrowing the dragons on the last quest. He looked at her as he said, "Did I not say the last time that dragons are sacred creatures, and it was an abomination to allow outsiders to borrow them? Look what happened. We lost our most promising young rider and her dragon. Now, they return, asking for our help yet again. They want another dragon and rider to accompany them on their latest quest. On top of that, they wish to borrow one of our weapons. They said that after the last quest, we would have a hundred years of peace. Yet, here we are. Who's to say when it will truly end? Should we sacrifice another of our own to this non-sense? I vote no."

Another councilman rose, "I agree. We cannot forfeit our own, or allow sacred dragon rider property to be borrowed freely."

"Everyone," Kirstiana said, "We are only voting on whether to allow them to borrow Ezmyra's talon, now. We shall take a separate vote for whether we allow them a warrior. Any arguments solely against the borrowing of the talon?"

No one else spoke up.

"Very well," she continued, "Those in favor of allowing them to borrow the talon?"

Most of the hands went up.

"Those opposed?"

Only a few hands rose.

Kirstiana gave a nod, "It's settled, then. Permission granted to borrow Ezmyra's talon."

Celestia felt a wave of relief wash over her that they would be allowed to take the talon. They had two of the five weapons. Now, they just needed the warrior.

"On the matter of appointing a dragon and rider to accompany them, do we have any further counter-arguments?"

"Yes," a councilwoman said, "Riders have chosen to live apart. We involve ourselves in the wars and problems of no one. Now, we have bent to the will of The Oracle, and gotten involved in these quests. We have sacrificed enough on the behalf of others."

"On the behalf of others?" Bridgot said suddenly, rising, "As if this matter doesn't concern you, too! Is this how you honor your fallen heroes?

Did you not hear us when we said that their sacrifice will have been for nothing if we fail? Is that what you want?"

Just then, they heard a crash outside. Kirstiana opened a portal with her magic, allowing them to view what was happening. As she did, Celestia could see the cause of the noise. Another star had fallen, right in the dragon rider city.

"You see?" Bridgot continued, "We have until the last star falls to complete this quest. Two of seven have already fallen!"

Kirstiana waved her hand, "King Bridgot. You have made your point. Do not forget that you are not a rider. The decision rests with this council. Now, any other count-"

"Dacron and Vondreer," Celestia said, rising.

"I beg your pardon?" Kirstiana said, confused.

"Dacron and Vondreer," she repeated, "A rider and dragon of yours. They battled a dark wizard. I read about them in your Hall of Weapons. They fought to save the world from a powerful dark wizard. They weren't thinking of only riders; they were thinking of all people. You hail them as heroes. Do you not find what they did to be noble?"

The council members stirred.

"Any further counter-arguments?" Kirstiana asked.

An elderly councilwoman rose, "Dacron and Vondreer were riders long ago, back when we were involved in the affairs of the world. They were heroes of their time. Since, we have chosen to butt out. The argument for their comparison to current events is irrelevant."

"Others?" Kirstiana asked once more.

No one said anything further.

"Very well," she said, sighing, "Then, it is finally time for the vote. Those in favor?"

A good number of them raised their hands.

"Those opposed?"

The rest raised their hands.

"The vote is close," Kirstiana said, "But, by one, we have a verdict. We will not send another dragon and rider to their deaths on this quest." As Celestia and her warriors started to object, she cut them off, "That is the final decision of this council. Take the talon and set out at dawn. Meeting adjourned."

The Brothers

4

When the first rays of the morning sun streamed through the green walls of the palace, the four of them set out. Frustration welled up inside of Celestia. *How can that be their decision?* she thought. Everyone seemed to be sharing her thoughts, as she looked from Thaandor to Kgansten to Bridgot. They rode their horses back out of the land of the dragon riders, through the border, and back into the grassy plain of the wizard realm.

They rode through Abyumo, each of them lost in their own frustration. When they stopped to make camp that night, Kgansten asked, "So, where are we headed? Korga, to find the dwarven weapon?"

"No," Thaandor said, "We must first go to Khanjgi, and find the ritual object which conceals Nazirdok's powers."

"Why would we find that first, with no way to destroy it, yet?" Bridgot asked.

"Because we are all at risk until it is safely in our possession."

Celestia shot him a look of confusion and concern, "How?"

"Since the powers do not have a body of their own, anyone who comes in contact with the ritual object is at risk. The powers will transplant themselves into them, taking them over like a possessing spirit. With a body, it will mean the virtual return of Nazirdok. We have to find it as soon as possible to avoid that happening. We'll keep it with us until the time comes to destroy it."

Their eyes widened as Celestia exclaimed, "Why didn't we go there first? We've put this whole quest in jeopardy by delaying!"

"Relax," Thaandor said, "It was a risk, but a necessary one. If we had gone there first, we would've had to backtrack all this way to get the wizard and dragon rider weapons. Think of the time we would have wasted. We were closer to those things, so we gathered them first. Now, everything we need is to the east. We'll collect the object in Khanjgi, and then journey south through the land of the dwarves, and the land of the elves. After that, we must search the vastness of the human realm for the final weapon to destroy it with."

Celestia nodded.

"The final weapon could be anywhere," Bridgot said anxiously, "The human realm is the largest, spanning countless lands. How can we hope to find it in time? We must search as we go."

"We don't have the time," Thaandor said, "Every second we waste is another chance of that object being found before we can get to it."

"We don't have the time *not* to," he countered, "What if the weapon is in one of the human lands we're journeying through? We'll have to come all the way back to find it. It will surely be too late."

"Bridgot's right," Kgansten said, "It's just like how we went first to find the wizard weapon and the dragon rider weapon. A risk, but necessary if we are to make it in time."

Thaandor sighed, "We shall allow the queen to decide."

They all looked at Celestia. She was silent a moment, considering their situation. On the one hand, she didn't want to take the risk that the object would be discovered before they could reach it. On the other hand, she knew they were right: if they waited to search for the human weapon, it would be too late. She looked at them as she said, "We shall search anything that's on the way. We won't go out of the way to search. We need to make it to Khanjgi as quickly as possible. However, I do agree that starting the search now will only help us."

Everyone was silent, looking at the ground. After a long pause, Thaandor said, "Very well. Everyone get some rest. We shall journey through Cardeas, Fluorasti, and Mashang to get to Kogatsa, as you did on the last quest. If the weapon is in one of those lands, we'll find it."

They journeyed northeast, cutting through a corner of Gachichken. It was uninhabited, with nowhere they could search for weapons. They made camp there, ready to venture into Cardeas the following day. As Celestia set up for her shift, Kgansten came up to sit beside her. After a pause, he said, "Bridgot loves you, you know."

She looked at him, surprised, "I know."

"You were stir crazy once," he paused, "You ran away. And you found yourself. Maybe that's what he needs right now. This quest came at the right time. For me as well . . ."

She sighed, "I suppose it's hard to accept now, since we're supposed to be happy. We're married, we have two kids, it's supposed to be 'happily ever after,' I guess. Knowing that his life with me is boring . . . I guess I feel like it's my fault."

"Of course not," Kgansten said, touching her arm, "You're the best thing that ever happened to him."

She looked away.

"You didn't do anything wrong," he said, "You're not the cause of his boredom. Trust me, I know. I'm in the same boat he is. I love my wife. I love my children. I wouldn't change them for the world. But, life has gotten stale and stagnant. It's about me, not them. I need to find myself again. I think he does, too."

"Perhaps you're right, Kgansten," Celestia said, turning toward him, "But, I just can't shake the feeling. I asked him to be king. I knew what I was signing up for. He didn't."

He sighed, "I know. But, you didn't force him. He made the decision on his own. He chose to be king. Not because he knew what he was in for, and thought he'd make a good king, but because he loved you, he wanted to be with you, and he knew you'd make a great queen."

She gave him a half-smile, "Thanks, Kgansten."

He patted her arm, "Goodnight, lassie."

With that, he lied down to get some rest, leaving her alone with her thoughts.

The next day, they crossed the border into Cardeas, heading east. *Nastazya's homeland*, Celestia thought. It was a beautiful, green country, full of forests and prairies.

"This way," Thaandor said suddenly.

They shot him questioning looks, following.

"Cardeas has a weapons depository this way. Perhaps the human weapon is there."

It took them most of the day, but they reached it. It wasn't much—a simple tin structure—but it contained a long row of famous weapons, held in regard by the people of Cardeas. They went in, looking at the various swords, bows and arrows, crossbows, and spears.

"It's not here," Celestia said, her blonde waves flowing around her, "I feel nothing." Her blue eyes showed her disappointment.

Her warriors sighed, Kgansten tugging at his red beard, Thaandor adjusting his pointed hat, and Bridgot's gray eyes meeting her own. After a pause, he said, "Well, it was worth a try."

Just then, the tin shack started to rock back and forth. As they scrambled to keep their feet, a group of cloaked men clambered along the walls above them, leaping down and yanking bags over their heads. Before they could get their bearings, they were knocked unconscious.

When she woke, Celestia was in a dimly lit room of stone. It looked very much like a dungeon. The bag was no longer over her head, but she could see that her warriors still had bags over their heads. They were chained to the wall on either side of her. There were five cloaked men standing before her, waiting for her to regain consciousness.

"What brings you here?" the leader demanded, "Who sent you?"

"Who are you people?" she asked groggily, holding her head.

"Answer the question," he snapped, unsheathing his sword and pointing it at her.

"I am Queen Celestia," she said, "Formerly, the princess of the prophecy. These are my warriors: my husband, King Bridgot, my mentor, Thaandor the wizard, and Kgansten the Dwarf Lord. Now, I ask you again: who are *you*?"

"Princess of the prophecy, you say?"

She nodded.

"Then, you knew my sister," he said. With that, he flung his hood back, revealing his dark-skinned face.

She looked at him carefully, studying him, before she said, "You're Nastazya's brothers, aren't you?"

Instead of answering, the rest of them removed their hoods. They all had brown eyes and black hair, with similar facial features. Three of the five had beards, and two of those had shaven heads, including the leader. One of the ones with no beard had long dreadlocks. They each had a piercing with a golden ring in a different place. The one with dreads had it on his nose. The leader had it on his left ear. One had it on his right ear, one on his lip, and one on his eyebrow. After a long pause, the leader sheathed his sword, saying, "Release them."

The other brothers unshackled her warriors and removed the bags from their heads. Bridgot, Kgansten, and Thaandor jumped up, trying to fight their captors.

"No! Stop!" Celestia yelled.

The brothers fought them off with ease, knocking them to the ground.

She marveled at how they were able to fight three such incredible warriors as though they were nothing. "How did you do that?" she asked.

The leader looked at her, "We drugged the four of you. It temporarily knocked you out. Until the effects wear off, you will all be weak and disoriented."

"Why did you do that?"

"We had to make sure you weren't spies. The land of Cardeas is at war with the north of Gachichken. We saw you come up from there, and then found you scrounging around our weapons depository. If you're not spies, what were you doing there?"

Celestia looked at each of the five of them before answering, "We are on another quest. The first was incomplete. If we fail, your sister will have given her life for nothing." She looked away sadly. When she looked back, they all wore solemn expressions.

"What can we do to help?" the leader asked.

She looked at them again, "We need to get to Khanjgi as quickly as possible, and we need to find a certain weapon of human make to fulfill the prophecy with. We thought perhaps it was in your weapons depository, but it's not there."

He looked down, sighing. After a pause, he said, "We shall provide you room and board tonight. Tomorrow, we shall guide you on the safest path out of Cardeas. Once you reach the border of Fluorasti, you're on your own."

"Thank you," she said.

He nodded.

The brothers helped them up off the ground, taking them up a stair-case, and into a wooden house through a trap door in the floor. It was quaint and cozy, and just large enough to house ten people comfortably. She guessed the five brothers had lived there with their parents and sister for years, before their mother passed away, and their sister left to become a dragon rider.

"You never told us your names," Celestia said once they had covered the trap door with a rug.

"I am Jacobi," the leader said, "And, this is Theodonis, Chiumbo, Ajala, and Thabiti." He gestured to each of his brothers as he said their names. Theodonis was the other brother with a beard and shaved head. Chiumbo had the dreads. Ajala had short hair and no beard, and Thabiti had a beard and short hair.

"Pleasure to meet all of you," she said.

Jacobi nodded, smiling, and they helped them back to a couple of spare bedrooms. Celestia's legs felt like rubber, and it was difficult for her to limp along. She hadn't fully felt the effects of being drugged until she'd tried to stand.

"Rest now," Chiumbo said, as they helped them lie down in the beds.

It was easier than Celestia expected, as her head hit the pillow and sleep overtook her.

As the light of dawn crept over the land of Cardeas, Thabiti came to wake them. They climbed upon their horses and rode off, away from the little wooden house, and into the forest. The brothers led them on a path hidden from view of the main road. It was a few more days through Cardeas, and they fully intended to accompany them to the border of Fluorasti.

As they were trotting along, they caught glimpses of the war camps on either side of the forest. Gachichken to the south, and Cardeas to the north. They were large armies, as they were made up of multiple kingdoms. Celestia looked worriedly at Nastazya's brothers. They had already lost her on their first quest. She didn't intend to lose them, too. She knew they had to destroy Nazirdok's powers before it was too late. Only that could stop the war, and keep them out of harm's way. As if the falling stars and the time limit on borrowing the wand of Merlin weren't enough motivation for moving quickly, this made it all the more real.

"We'll have to move swiftly and stealthily," Jacobi said, "if we want to get you through unnoticed."

They all nodded, riding through the forest as quickly as they reasonably could. They rode all day, until Ajala found a spot to make camp. They dismounted, caring for their steeds, and preparing a quick meal. Once they all settled in, Jacobi and Theodonis took the first watch. Chiumbo and Thabiti were next, and then Ajala and Bridgot. They were rotating shifts of three pairs each night, so everyone could also get a full night of sleep in. It would take almost a week to complete their journey to Fluorasti, and depart from Nastazya's brothers.

The nine of them journeyed together, moving through the forest by day, and sleeping in shifts by night. Celestia was getting used to the routine of the road again, as she had been on their first quest. The brothers had been nice enough to refill their saddlebags before they left their house, but a week was plenty of time for them to deplete, especially when they weren't able to stop in any towns on the way, for fear of discovery or attack.

One night, as she was taking her shift with Jacobi, she asked, "So, where is your father? I had hoped to meet him. He gave such a beautiful speech at Nastazya's funeral."

He faltered, looking away, "He passed away a couple years after Nastazya. Combination of old age and a broken heart."

She looked down sadly, "Oh. I'm sorry."

"Me, too," he said, "He was a good man." After a pause, he added, "He was a good father."

Celestia touched his arm sympathetically.

"Now, it's just my brothers and me," he continued, blinking away the almost-tears, "We're Cardeas' best warriors. We'll be summoned into this war when they need it most. In the meantime, we're watching the perimeter, to ensure no spies from Gachichken slip through."

"So who's watching it now, then?" she asked.

"We assigned some of our young warrior apprentices to the detail until we get back."

She nodded.

Jacobi turned to look at her, a strange expression on his face. It seemed an eternity before he spoke, but she dared not say anything. "What was your experience with my sister?" he asked.

"What do you mean?"

"I mean, what was she like?" he said.

Celestia looked at him questioningly, "You don't know?"

"I knew her growing up," he replied, "But, once she left home and became a rider . . . well, I'm sure she changed."

She gave him a nod of understanding, "She was amazing. We were all blown away by her. She was strong, confident, brave, loyal, skilled, and powerful. I'd never met anyone like her before. I like to think of her as my friend. I think she would have agreed. She cared for all of us, and we for her. She told me the story of how she became a rider, and the special bond she shared with Ezmyra. She even found love on our quest, with our elven warrior, Aurano. They planned on being together when the quest was over. They just . . . never got the chance." Celestia looked away sadly, thinking of how her friends never got their shot at happily ever after.

Jacobi's eyes widened, "My sister was in love with an elf?"

She returned her gaze to him, "And he with her. The day she died, she was fending off some faeries with her magic, along with the help of her dragon. She gave us the chance to complete our quest. Without her, we never would have made it into the city. Aurano didn't want to leave her, but she told him she'd follow, and then she pulled the lever that would release the barrels we were in downstream into the city. She didn't jump into her barrel. She saved our lives, sacrificing her own. Later on, Aurano was killed as well. He jumped in front of me and took a curse, so I could fulfill the prophecy. We buried them side by side."

He allowed a single tear to flow from his eyes, looking at her with more tears frozen in place, refusing to fall.

"Your sister was a hero," she said.

He nodded, "Yes, she was. I think I understand her better now." After a pause, he added, "Thank you." He wiped the tears from his eyes, letting out a shaky breath.

Celestia reached over, touching his shoulder, "Believe me, I know what it means to learn about someone you love whom you didn't have the chance to fully know."

In that moment, she felt such a mixture of emotion, she found it difficult to hold back her own tears. It had been almost ten years since that fateful day, and yet thinking of it now, she felt the grief just as strongly.

"We should wake Theodonis and Thaandor for their shift," he said.

She nodded in agreement, and they did so, settling in for the night to sleep.

Their time traveling with the brothers was a breeze. They made it through Cardeas quickly and efficiently. It was probably the easiest and most secure journey Celestia had ever been a part of, apart from journeys taken in the royal caravan.

As they reached the border of Fluorasti, Jacobi said, "It was an honor to escort the friends of our sister."

"The honor was ours," Celestia replied.

As she reached over to hug him, a spear flew between them.

"Down!" he shouted, ducking and hurrying to unsheathe his sword. Everyone scrambled to get behind the cover of the trees and arm themselves.

Celestia peered around the tree and saw soldiers approaching. They were human men, garbed in armor, running toward them, yelling. She leaned back against the tree, breathing slow, and feeling the smooth wood of her bow, and the feathered end of her arrow between her fingers. She looked over at the others, nodding. Then, she ran out from behind the tree, firing arrows at the oncoming ambush. She shot down several of them, ducking behind the next tree. Bridgot and Nastazya's brothers did the same, thinning them out. Kgansten had to wait for them to get closer, as he had no skill with a bow. Thaandor used his staff to wipe them out by magic.

Once they neared them, they put away the bows and arrows and unsheathed their swords. Kgansten leapt out, swinging his axe. Thaandor continued to use his staff to thin them out. Celestia swung her sword, engaging the soldiers. It had been a long time since she'd fought a real opponent. She'd barely practiced, since they were supposed to enjoy peace in the land for the rest of their lives. She hadn't figured she'd have need of it. She couldn't keep up as she once did, and the soldier she was fighting knocked her back, forcing her to fight from the ground. She struggled to reach her feet as she fought, but she fell again. He smiled, seeing he had the upper hand. He swung hard and knocked the sword from her hand.

Celestia knew her moment had come. She closed her eyes, bracing herself for his final blow. Suddenly, she heard Bridgot yelling, and she opened her eyes to see him swing his sword, blocking the soldier's blow and knocking him backward. He ran his blade through his gut, killing him. She breathed a sigh of relief, grabbing her sword and getting up.

"I'm a little rusty!" she said, positioning herself behind him.

"Don't worry, I've got your back!" he shouted.

They fought the next wave that came their way side-by-side and back-to-back; twirling, thrusting, and parrying. Celestia's muscle memory came back to her, and she began to fight them off with ease.

"Celestia!" Thaandor yelled, "I know it's not the best time, but I'd like to teach you a new spell!"

"What?" she shouted back.

"Use your wand! Focus on your opponents and aim at them," he said, ducking around the trees and blasting the soldiers with his staff, "Think about getting them away from you. It's more complex than other spells you've learned, but try it! The incantation is *harrow!*"

She sliced her sword through the soldier she was fighting, giving her a small window of opportunity. She pulled her wand from her gown and aimed it at the soldiers that were coming her way. Focusing on them, she thought of getting them away from her and Bridgot. "*Harrow!*" she shouted. Blue magic streamed from her wand, knocking the group of soldiers back.

"Good!" he yelled, "Now, try another spell. Eventually, once you're in tune with your powers, you won't need to recite the words—only think of what they need to do. For now, the words will help you direct and control your magic. So, this time, when you focus on them, think of shooting them with arrows. Say *depugno!*"

Celestia focused in on them again, as they got up from where she'd knocked them back. She aimed her wand and thought of how she would thin them out with her bow and arrow, "*Depugno!*"

This time, when the magic hit them, they were all run through, as though they'd been hit with arrows, straight through their armor. She was awed and horrified at the same time. She looked at Thaandor, eyes wide.

He nodded, "Now, you see. The only thing separating a good wizard from a bad one is their individual intent. We have the power to deal out death and destruction. When and how we choose to use our powers is what defines us. It's what separates wizards like me from wizards like Nazirdok. Which side you will choose is up to you."

Thaandor continued making his way across the battlefield as more soldiers made their way up to Bridgot and her. She tucked the wand back in her dress, returning to her sword. She could see Kgansten making his way through the onslaught with his axe. Nastazya's brothers were fighting all around them, taking down the soldiers with ease.

The ambush was thinned down to a handful of men. The cowards began to retreat, leaving only the diehards still fighting. Celestia saw Kgansten struggling against a group of soldiers, and hurried to his aid, cutting several of them down.

"Thanks," he said, continuing to fight, "These bastards were almost getting tough."

She laughed, blocking another soldier's blow. As they fought together, she looked back to see how Bridgot was doing. To her horror, she could see that he was being backed toward the edge of a nearby ravine. She pulled out her wand, aiming it at the group she and Kgansten were fighting, and yelled, "*Depugno!*"

Once they had fallen, she hurried back across the battlefield to Bridgot. She aimed her wand at the group around him, but she wasn't sure if the spell would hit him, too. She shouted, "*Harrow!*" and knocked them down instead.

When she looked again, there were still two soldiers standing, both of them fighting Bridgot. She ran over, pointing her sword at the two remaining soldiers. One of them knocked Bridgot down, and started to swing his sword down upon him as he tried to regain his footing. She swung her sword faster, fighting him off and killing him. The other one engaged her, and she fought him back as Bridgot reached his feet. She knocked the sword from his hand and sheathed her own, pointing her wand at him instead.

He laughed, "What are you going to do with that? Shoot me with imaginary arrows like you did to my men?"

"No," she said, looking down.

He followed her gaze to his feet, realizing he was standing at the edge of the ravine. He looked up in panic.

"*Harrow,*" she said.

The magic streamed from her wand once more, knocking him back, right off the edge. The rest of the soldiers fled as she turned back to Bridgot, "No, *I've* got *your* back."

Bridgot gave his wife a weak smile, dropping to his knees. Celestia could see he'd been stabbed in his side. He lifted his hand, seeing it was covered in blood, and looked up at her sorrowfully. Her eyes widened, and she rushed to his side, "You're going to be alright. It's nothing."

Nastazya's brothers and Kgansten gathered around them, tears forming in their eyes. They stood there, helplessly watching. Celestia began to panic as she saw the tears start to spill over the Dwarf Lord's rough, ruddy cheeks, and into his copper beard. She looked back at Bridgot, thinking, *No . . .*

Raw Power

5

"Move!" Thaandor shouted, pushing through them. When he saw Bridgot, he knelt beside him, turning to Celestia. "It's time to learn your next spell," he said.

She looked back at him with uncertainty, unable to move.

"You must focus on the wound, observe the damages to the body, and visualize the way it's supposed to be. When you're ready, place your hand over the wound, and recite the incantation, *shuleas*."

"I don't think I can," she said, panicked, "What if I screw it up?"

"You can do this," he said, "Just focus."

She nodded, forcing herself to look at Bridgot's wound, and focus on it. Then, she pictured how it was supposed to look and placed her hand upon it. She could feel him wince upon contact, but he sucked in a breath, holding it as he waited. She centered herself as she said, "*Shuleas*."

To everyone's amazement, her blue magic radiated from her hand into the stab wound. It glowed until she lifted her hand. When she did, the hole in Bridgot's side was gone. The blood remained—the only evidence of what had been there.

Bridgot's eyes widened, "You did it! That was incredible!"

Celestia breathed a sigh of relief, sitting on the ground.

"Are you alright?" he asked, "You don't look so good."

"She exhausted a lot of power today," Thaandor said, "It drains your energy the same as doing those things manually. Healing is very complex, and thus, requires a good deal of energy. She needs rest to recover."

"We will watch over you as you rest tonight," Jacobi said, "Tomorrow, we will go our separate ways. You all need to get to Khanjgi. We need to get home. If that ambush from Gachichken came for us here, I'm betting the armies of Cardeas need us now."

"Thank you," Bridgot said.

Jacobi nodded.

Chiumbo and Thabiti helped Bridgot and Celestia to their feet, guiding them to where they would make camp.

"You did well today," Thaandor said to Celestia as they walked, "You learned how to knock back enemies, how to shoot them with magical arrows in the course of combat, and how to heal flesh wounds. I daresay you've learned more today than in all your training thus far. I'm sorry that it happened during the course of an actual battle. I shall continue your training as we travel, and hopefully prepare you enough for whatever we may face along the way."

She nodded wearily.

As they reached the campsite—a secluded clearing just beyond the battle site—Bridgot and Celestia collapsed to the ground beside each other. Bridgot reached over, brushing his fingers against Celestia's hand. "Thank you," he whispered, "You saved my life today."

She allowed him to take her hand in his, and a smile spread across her face. In spite of everything, she knew their love was alive, and that was all that mattered as she drifted off to sleep.

When they woke, the brothers were already gone.

"Ready?" Thaandor asked. He and Kgansten were already saddling the horses.

Bridgot and Celestia got up slowly, gathering their bearings. She fumbled about, a little disoriented. Sleep had helped her recover her strength. Bridgot clutched his side as he rose, still feeling the effects of being stabbed. They walked over to Samson and Razel's sides, climbing upon their backs.

The four of them continued their journey through Fluorasti, riding all day through the trees. Fluorasti was full of ravines near the forest, like the one they had fought by on the border. It wasn't as green as Cardeas, but it was still lush with life. Celestia was reminded of the forests of Millhaymae, which she and Bridgot had traveled through on their first quest. Though it wasn't the fondest memory, as they had been captured by slave traders there, she remembered how she and Bridgot had felt then. They had just begun to develop feelings for one another—not yet in love, but falling. It gave her butterflies in her stomach, and she looked over at him. He shot her a smile, gray eyes twinkling, brown curls bobbing against his head as he rode upon Samson's back. She looked away, blushing. She wasn't sure why, but she felt a renewed sense of romance between them.

When they stopped to make camp that night, Bridgot and Kgansten chatted over dinner, as Thaandor worked on Celestia's training.

"I'll teach you one spell a night," Thaandor said, "But first, why don't you show me the spells you've been practicing?"

She nodded, proceeding to show him the spells he had taught her over the course of time since the last quest. She knew spells that would sweep the floor, move objects, cure a cold, dust furniture, steam garments, clean skin and hair, heal cuts and bruises, bloom flowers, and produce water. She amazed herself with how easy it was to cast them when she used her wand compared to simply her hands.

"Excellent," he said when she was finished, "You have them down."

"Yes," Celestia replied, "I've had plenty of time to practice."

"I think that's enough of a drain for you tonight," he said, "Tomorrow, I will teach you something new."

She nodded, "Very well."

When she curled up to sleep, she thought about all the spells she had learned already, and realized just how much she still had to learn. Most of the spells she knew weren't useful in combat or healing. Most of them were useful around the house. With a quest of such importance on the line, she knew one spell a night would barely prepare her for what they might face. She sighed, wondering if they could really destroy his powers in time. *There's an idea*, she thought, *If there were a spell to make us faster or give us more time, that would be the one to learn. At the very least, one which could help us find the weapon . . .*

The next few nights, Celestia learned how to produce fire, how to produce heat, how to heal bones, how to remove poison, and how to create a protective barrier for herself and others.

"This one will be particularly difficult to master," Thaandor said.

"More difficult than learning how to mend bones without a broken bone to practice on?" she laughed.

"Let us hope you don't have to use that spell on someone's bones," he replied, perpetuating the serious nature of their lessons, "To form a barrier of protection, you must feel your own magic coursing through your veins. Once you've tuned into the current, you must create a desire to protect yourself and possibly others. Try to pretend that someone is attacking you. Use your fear to create this desire. When you have it, wave your arm and say, *Cerco*."

Celestia focused within herself, trying to feel her magic. It was faint, and she had difficulty tuning into it. It was like a vague taste in your mouth that you couldn't fully identify. It kept slipping away each time she thought she felt it.

"Magic is part of all of us who possess the gift," Thaandor said, "It courses through your veins as it has since you got your powers. Remember the feeling you had when you first got them . . . remember how the magic burst from you, and you could feel the sensation all through you."

She stopped trying to concentrate, and allowed herself to recall the way she'd felt then. Nazirdok was trying to destroy them and complete his ritual for power, and she knew she had to stop him, but she couldn't. Suddenly, she felt her powers coursing through her veins, and she knew she was aglow once more. The desire to protect herself came easily, and she opened her eyes, waving her wand and saying, "*Cerco*."

A shimmering wall of blue energy appeared around her, and she could see the look of astonishment on Thaandor's face. He snapped out of it, ordering Bridgot and Kgansten to attack the wall with sword and axe. They did so, and not one of their blows was able to penetrate the wall. Thaandor produced several magical attacks, and not even they could break down her barrier.

Finally, Thaandor nodded, and Celestia released her hold. The wall disappeared into a mist, and the three men stared at her in awe. She did not understand their astonishment, as all she'd done was learned another spell. She looked down as the blue sparks of power vanished from her fingertips.

Everyone was silent for a moment before Thaandor said, "This is beyond anything I've ever seen. No one has ever been able to perform that spell on the first try . . . at least, not to that degree." His eyes were still wide with astonishment as he stared at her.

Bridgot and Kgansten shared his expression. They dropped their weapons to the ground beside them, not saying anything.

After a pause, Celestia said, "What do you mean 'not to that degree?'"

Thaandor cleared his throat, snapping out of his trance, "You're more powerful than I ever imagined. You have no idea what you did, do you?"

She shook her head, "I learned another spell. I felt my magic coursing through me, as you said to do, and I created a protective barrier, as the spell was to be used for."

He mimicked her head shaking as he said, "Your power level increased exponentially. It was higher than our leader and most powerful councilman, Thrindil. Your powers surged higher than should be possible. I daresay you may have approached the level of Merlin himself."

"What?" she replied, awestruck, "How? It was no different from when I got my powers the first time. I did what you said, and thought of how I felt then, and how my powers felt when they first coursed through me."

"Your entire body glowed with your power. I've never seen that happen past when a wizard first gets them. Even your eyes glowed blue. Not only that, but you were able to sustain it, and wield your barrier against an onslaught of weapons *and* magic. I used advanced spells designed to tear down a wizard's barrier, but none worked."

"What?" she said again, "How is that possible?"

"I don't know," he replied, "I have no answers for this. But, perhaps it is how you were able to defeat Nazirdok."

She looked away, wondering. The Oracle had not given her a clear answer, and if Thaandor wasn't sure what happened, she didn't know if The Oracle even *could* answer her.

"Do you feel a drain?" Thaandor asked suddenly.

Celestia thought about it a moment. She didn't feel the normal wave of exhaustion she felt after performing rigorous magic. She shook her head.

His eyes widened even more, and she thought they might pop out of his head. After another long pause, he said, "Let's all get some rest. I don't know what this means, but I need sleep before I can think too much on it."

They all settled into the soft grass, and Celestia took the first watch. She was wide awake, and she had no idea how any of this was possible. She stared into the night as her warriors slept, thinking, *What is this power? How can I control it?*

The next day, everyone rode quietly, shooting sideways glances at Celestia. She could feel their eyes boring into her, and the judgment of those who were her loyal warriors made her uncomfortable. She kept looking at her hands as she rode, amazed by the visible magic she had seen coming from them. The day was long and hot, and by the end of it, they were all ready to make camp.

As they ate their stew in silence, sitting upon a few logs they'd found, they continued to stare at her. Finally, Thaandor broke the silence, "I consulted with The Oracle during my shift last night, and she told me more about your powers. You haven't yet discovered what all you can do. Most wizards are never able to reach their full potential, as they are unable to tap into their raw power. It bursts from us when we receive our powers and don't yet understand them or know how to control them. But, after that point, we can never truly use them to their fullest extent. You have somehow discovered how to tap into your raw power and wield it with control. There have only been six other wizards in history who've been able to do the same, including Merlin."

Celestia took a minute to process what he was saying, "So, I tapped into my raw power, and can wield it, making me more powerful than I normally could be?"

"Yes," he answered, "Yet still, I must somehow be the one to train you. There are no wizards alive with your ability. So, I can only teach you what I know. The rest you must figure out for yourself."

"How am I to figure out how to wield such powers on my own?"

"Wizards had to start somewhere," he replied, "How do you think the first wizards learned how to control their powers? Magic is all about intent; what do you *intend* to do with it? Decide that, and you won't need lessons and spells. You'll need only yourself—your heart and your mind—to guide you."

She thought about it for a while, still trying to process everything. The Oracle knew *what* had happened, but nobody could tell her *why*. "Did Nazirdok have this ability?" she asked.

"No," Thaandor said, "What would make you think that?"

"How did he have so much more power than even that of a dragon rider, then?"

He smiled, understanding what she was asking, "As you know, wizards are limited by their bodies as far as how much power we can use, based on the amount of energy a spell takes to conjure, and how much that energy usage drains us."

"Yes," Celestia affirmed.

"Well, there are other sources we can use for energy. If we were able to tap into a wellspring of energy, our powers would not have such limits."

She paused, "Are you saying he had an unlimited energy supply?"

"Not unlimited," he answered, "But with a far greater limit than simply the limit of his own body."

"How?" Bridgot asked suddenly.

"Yes, I'm curious as well," Kgansten said, scratching his red hair beneath his helmet.

Celestia smiled with relief that they were engaging in the conversation, rather than still staring at her in astonishment.

"There are two possibilities. One: other living things. Anything and anyone with a life force has energy. It is possible for a wizard to tap into the life forces of others. They could be beings such as humans, elves, dwarves, etc. Or, they could even be plants and animals. That's why dragon riders are more powerful than wizards; they can tap into the power of their dragons," Thaandor said, looking at each of them in turn.

"So, what's the second possibility?" Bridgot asked.

Thaandor looked at him then, "There are magic storage units of sorts—another of Merlin's inventions—in which wizards can stockpile their powers. Each night, before they sleep and recover their full strength, they could put their unused energy from the day into a storage unit. After a while, you would have a great reserve from which you could draw energy when needed. These storage units can easily be concealed in any common object, from a ring to a sword to a crystal ball. Other wizards could even do the same, if they were his allies, giving him even greater reserves. Or worse, dragons could put their energy inside. Truly, that would be as close to limitless power as you could get."

"So, what sort of energy reserves does raw power give you?" Celestia asked.

"I don't know," he said, looking at her, "I've never met anyone who could wield it. If I had to guess, perhaps energy equal to that of a dragon. I couldn't say for certain. I'm afraid you'll have to discover your own limits."

Celestia twisted a strand of white-blonde hair nervously, looking around at the faces of her warriors. Their beards had all grown longer on the road. For Kgansten and Thaandor, that meant very little. For Bridgot, it meant that he desperately needed a trim.

"Tomorrow, we shall visit Fluorasti's Great Hall of Weapons," Thaandor said, "and see if the human weapon is there."

"No," Celestia said, "Let's not waste our time. It's not there."

They were all silent a moment before Bridgot said, "What do you mean? How do you know?"

"I don't know," she responded, "I just . . . sense it. I can *feel* that it isn't there."

"My God," Thaandor said, "Your range has increased as exponentially as your powers."

"What are you talking about?" Kgansten asked.

"The range in which she can sense the required weapons," he replied. He paused, muttering, "This is incredible."

"You can sense all the way to their Hall of Weapons?" Bridgot asked.

Celestia nodded, "I can feel that the weapon isn't in Fluorasti."

"That's amazing!" Kgansten said, "This quest just got a whole lot simpler."

"It's not in Cardeas, Gachichken, or Mashang, either," she added.

"That's impossible," Thaandor said, "No one's range is that large."

"Apparently, a lot of things happening within me are impossible," Celestia said, "But, they're happening nonetheless."

They journeyed the rest of the way across Fluorasti, with Thaandor cautiously training Celestia on basic spells the whole way. She learned spells for cushioning the ground, producing food, and even a much-needed hair grooming spell. She was able to use it to cut and brush everyone's hair and beards. With magic, it was unnecessary to risk stopping in villages along the way. They could keep everyone clean, fed, and comfortable with spells.

Despite the nightly magical education, it seemed an eternity to cross the expanse of Fluorasti, which was two-thirds the size of Gachichken. Somehow, they had crossed that on their last quest, and it hadn't felt quite so long as this. Though staying in a town wasn't necessary, the feeling of getting clean by magic wasn't as satisfying as actually washing. So, they decided to stop in a town one night, knowing they would cross the border into Mashang the next day, and, once there, it would be too great a risk to stop anywhere.

"Welcome to the Bungalow Inn!" an over-enthusiastic innkeeper greeted them. He was a middle-aged man with brown hair and brown eyes. He gestured grandly to a sign behind him as he spoke, which said *Bungalow Inn* on it. It was a larger inn than any they'd stayed in before, and Celestia was amazed. "To what do I owe the honor of royalty staying in my humble inn?" he asked.

"We're simply passing through, as any traveler," King Bridgot said, waving off his flattery.

"We only need two rooms for the night," Queen Celestia added.

"I get it," the innkeeper whispered, "Trying to blend in? Don't worry, to me you're common folk, like us." He winked, nudging Bridgot's arm.

"Great," Bridgot said, hiding his annoyance, "Can we get a room, please?"

"Of course!" he said, walking toward the staircase, "Right this way."

They followed him upstairs, and to two rooms across the hall from each other, "I'm sorry I don't have nicer rooms available. I can move some other guests around to get the suites for you if you like."

"No, these will do just fine," Celestia said quickly, "Thank you."

He bowed, heading back downstairs. As they were opening the doors, he poked his head around the corner, adding, "Washroom's just down here, at the top of the stairs. You're welcome to leave your clothes at the desk, and I'll have them washed and ready for you. Breakfast will be available in the morning, bright and early."

"Wonderful," Celestia said, nodding.

With that, he disappeared down the stairs. They shook their heads as Bridgot and Celestia entered one of the rooms, and Kgansten and Thaandor the other. It was a little wooden room with faded yellow bedding, a couple of nightstands, and a wardrobe. It reminded Celestia of many other inns they'd stayed at.

They all took turns washing up, and Celestia was relieved to actually feel water against her skin, and be able to wash herself. It was far more satisfying to clean her skin, hair, and teeth manually than by magic. Once they were clean, Kgansten delivered everyone's clothes to the desk, and they went back to their rooms.

"At least this time around, I don't have to feel guilty for sharing a bed with you," Bridgot said.

Celestia shook her head, giving him a wry smile, "No, I suppose you don't. Still, it almost feels the way it did then."

As they slipped into their nightclothes, Bridgot said, "For that, I'm glad. I miss those days."

"Me, too," she admitted, "Though, I understand my place, now. I'm not on this quest because I'm running away. It is my duty to finish what we started as much as it's my duty to rule our kingdom and raise our kids."

"I know," he said, looking down, "But, sometimes it's good to take a break from your duties. We all need that occasionally."

They climbed into the bed side-by-side, getting comfortable.

"I suppose you're right," Celestia said, "Though magic can make the ground feel more like a bed, nothing quite beats an actual bed." She nestled down into the mattress, feeling the blankets around her.

He smiled, the familiar twinkle in his gray eyes appearing.

She smiled back at him, scooting closer.

"No matter what happens, you'll always be my wife," he said, looking deep into her eyes, "Whatever life throws at me, I'll never stop loving you."

"It's amazing," she said, meeting his gaze.

"What?" he asked, puzzled.

"All this time and you still give me butterflies when you say things like that."

He leaned in, kissing her softly. She kissed him back eagerly, and they lost themselves in each other's sweet embrace.

When the sun's rays peeked through the window, Celestia awoke. She looked up at her husband, and the vulnerable innocence of his sleeping face. She smiled, feeling the warmth of his skin against her own, his arm stretched over her. It had been years since they'd fallen asleep holding each other. Her heart sang within her, indulging in the youthful feeling. Instead of getting up, she snuggled closer, turning her face into his chest. He smelled musky, yet fresh, like a campfire made from newly chopped wood. There were vague undertones of pine needles, mint, and sweat. Nothing quite compared to his scent. To her, it was the smell of home.

He sucked in a breath as he regained consciousness, stretching his arm above him, and opening his droopy eyes, "Good morning," he said, wrapping his arm around her.

"Good morning," she replied, smiling up at him.

He smiled back, kissing her forehead and settling back down. They lied like that for a while, before he said, "I suppose we should get some food and set out."

"I suppose so," she said, sighing.

They got up finally, getting dressed and heading down to get some food. Thaandor and Kgansten were already there, eating.

"Good morning," Kgansten said when he saw them, raising his glass.

"Sleep well?" Thaandor asked, smirking.

Bridgot and Celestia looked at each other. "Yes, quite," Bridgot said quickly, "What kinds of things do they have to eat?"

"We have the standard breakfast platter," the innkeeper answered, coming up behind them, "It has bacon, eggs, hash browns, and toast with a pint of orange juice."

"Sounds great," Celestia said, taking a seat.

Bridgot sat as well, and the innkeeper brought them a couple plates of food.

As they were eating, a familiar voice said, "Margarita? Is that you?"

On hearing her old alias, Celestia turned to see Irene, sitting at a nearby table.

"Margarita! Bridgot!" she yelled, coming over.

"Irene?" Celestia said, rising and hugging her, "I don't believe it!"

Irene had black hair, brown eyes, and a fair complexion. Celestia barely recognized her in regular clothes, rather than the servant's dress and bonnet she'd always seen her in. She was wearing a lovely, purple dress, with a gathered skirt and bustled rear. Her long, black hair was half up, half down, in loose curls.

"A queen?" Irene asked in disbelief, looking up at Celestia's silver crown.

"Oh," she said, touching her tiara, "Yes. I was born a princess. I was in disguise when you met me."

She continued to stare at her in disbelief.

"My name's not Margarita, by the way. It's Celestia—Queen Celestia of Ivétoiless."

"*I* wasn't lying when we met," Bridgot added, shaking her hand, "My name *is* Bridgot, and I *was* a peasant. Now, I'm her husband, and king of Ivétoiless."

"You weren't married then?" she asked.

"Oh, I guess I did lie, a little," he said, "No, we weren't married. But, we are now."

"Wow," Irene said, "King and queen. Celestia, huh? Wow."

"Sorry we lied," she inserted, "We didn't know who we could trust. I was a runaway, and we were on an important quest. I couldn't risk being sent home. Everyone was searching for me."

"It's alright," she said, composing herself, "I understand. I never fully revealed who I was, either. I'm a noblewoman of the court of Batosque, here in Fluorasti. I had been traveling with a few other nobles, and gotten separated from my group. As I was searching for them, the slave traders captured me. It turns out my family had sent out search parties after me, and they found me in the village after you liberated us. I thank you both for what you did."

"No need to thank us," Bridgot said, "We did what we had to do to get out of there."

"But, you didn't only think of yourselves," Irene responded, "You didn't have to, but you liberated us all. And, you stuck around to help an entire village learn to defend themselves." She looked down, "I'm humbled to be in the presence of two such heroes."

"It's good to see you," Celestia said, touching her arm, "I'm glad you found your way home."

She gave them a nod, turning back to her table. Before she sat, she added, "I shall tell Colleen of this next time I see her."

"You keep in contact?" she asked.

Irene smiled, "Of course. We were friends for quite a while. We write frequently, and I occasionally visit her village."

"Give her our best wishes when you tell her," she said.

Irene nodded, still smiling.

With that, the four of them gathered their belongings to set out again. They would cross the border into Mashang that day, and from there, it was two more weeks to Khanjgi. Celestia smiled to herself as they hopped upon their horses. *What are the chances of running into someone we know here?* she thought. It had been a long time since she'd thought of Colleen and Irene, and she missed them terribly. Though the circumstances of their meeting hadn't been ideal, she had formed friendships with the both of them. She hoped Colleen was doing well, and that her village was thriving in the aftermath of their liberation.

The chance meeting with their old friend, combined with the night she and Bridgot had shared at the inn, made her smile. The sun seemed brighter, the grass seemed greener, and the sky seemed bluer, as they rode through the day. Night settled in just as they crossed the border to Mashang, stopping to make camp. Right as she was thinking to herself, *Maybe we really* can *do this*, there was a streak of light on the horizon, followed by a loud explosion, as a star fell to the earth.

"A star!" Kgansten shouted as they all gasped.

"Three down, four to go," Thaandor said solemnly.

Kogatsa

6

As the red-orange light of the sun peeked over the horizon, they set out. Their levity from the day before was muddled, as they rode ahead, trying to pick up speed through their dismay. They weren't sure if they'd be able to complete the quest in time. They stuck to the shadows, not daring to stop in any more villages, especially there.

The land of Mashang was gray and cloudy, and they could barely see as they journeyed across it. It rained off and on as they rode, soaking them to the bone. Thaandor had to teach Celestia a few new spells, to keep everyone from getting sick.

"Wave your wand over our heads," he instructed, "And say, *Corsen*."

She did so, and a magical umbrella formed over and around the four of them and their horses, keeping up with them as they rode, and keeping them dry from the rain.

"Good," Thaandor continued, "Next, think about being warm and dry, and say, *Vera*."

Celestia pointed her wand at herself, repeating the incantation. Once she had, she watched in amazement as her skin and clothes dried themselves, the water slowly disappearing from her soaked gown, the clinging skirt releasing its grip. She felt warm and cozy, and she was completely dry. She did the same to Razel, and then to each of her warriors and their steeds.

Once they were all warm and dry, they were able to ride through the rain in peace, watching the gray droplets of water streak angrily across the barrier around them, creating a shimmering, misty rainbow inside. The sound of the rain was calming, except for the crashing thunder every so often. Lightning streaked across the sky ahead, and the world looked dark and gloomy, but they were safe and sound in their little pocket of protection.

There weren't any signs of life as they moved through the land. The forest was quiet, and they saw no towns or war camps nearby. They stuck close together, always on guard. They weren't sure how close to Kogatsa they would get before they ran into trouble. If things were still the same as they were on their first quest, then Mashang was an ally of Kogatsa, and therefore, enemy territory.

Things were sure to be different, however, since they'd destroyed Nazirdok. The kingdom of Khanjgi was under new leadership now. It was even possible they were in friendly territory. But, as Kogatsa was a land famous for producing dark wizards and creatures of darkness, it was unlikely. Chances were that they would face struggle and resistance as they tried to get the ritual object containing Nazirdok's powers.

They crossed Mashang in record time, taking only a week and a half to reach Kogatsa. Their path became quite familiar once they did. The dark, foggy woods were just as they remembered. They followed the same path, though it was faster and easier with their horses, rather than on foot. For that, Celestia was grateful, as these woods made her uneasy. They almost reached the ferry dock before they stopped to make camp.

"We'll be able to cross first thing in the morning," Thaandor said, "From there, it will be a short trip into Khanjgi."

"We'll have to be careful," Bridgot inserted, "There's no way to know whether it will be friendly territory."

"Something tells me it won't," Kgansten said.

"They were singing our praises when we left," Celestia retorted, "But, we don't know what has happened in the meantime. It's very possible that things could have gotten bad again. Wars have broken out all across the land. We have no way to know what awaits us."

"Crossing Mashang was almost too easy," Bridgot said, "It was like . . . no one was there. I fear Kogatsa will be much different."

"You're right," Kgansten agreed, "I hadn't thought about it until now. But, we didn't come across a single living soul. It was like a ghost town. None of our journeys have been that easy."

"Relax," Thaandor asserted, "before we get ahead of ourselves. There's no need to assume the worst. We must only be prepared for it."

"I agree," Celestia said, "Why don't we all get some rest. Bridgot and I will take the first shift. It's better to split the watches in pairs in these woods."

"Very well," Thaandor agreed. He and Kgansten lied down to sleep, as Celestia and Bridgot sat upon a mossy boulder to begin their watch.

"Bridgot, I have to ask you something," Celestia said, "And, I need you to answer honestly."

He looked at her earnestly, scratching his freshly-trimmed beard. After a moment, he asked, "What is it?"

"When you spoke to The Oracle this time, did she say anything about one of you dying?"

"No," he said, surprised, "Why? Did she say something to *you* about that?"

Celestia breathed a sigh of relief, "No. But, neither did she on our last quest. I had to be sure before crossing the ferry tomorrow." She looked down.

Bridgot took her hand, understanding, "We may be completing the old quest, but this is *not* the old quest."

"I know. Yet, the nearer we draw to Khanjgi, the more I think of what happened last time we were here, and the more I worry that something bad will happen again," she looked at him, "I almost lost you last time. And we did lose Nastazya, and Aurano."

"I know," he said, squeezing her hand, "But, we can't know what's going to happen. All we can do is fight our way through and pray for the best."

She looked away, trying to hide her tears from him.

He gently pulled her face back toward him, "The last time, I feared what might happen. Mostly because . . . I knew we couldn't be together, and I couldn't live with that. But now, here we are. Married. I'm not afraid of what might happen anymore. Everyone must reach their end at some point. All I know is that, if I reach mine, it won't be for nothing. I'll make it the most glorious end the world has ever known. I'll go down fighting. And that's enough for me."

Her tears streamed down as she said, "I'm not afraid of what might happen to me, or even to you. I fear for a life without you. I fear failing this quest. I fear what that would mean for our children, and for the world."

"Me, too," he said, "But, if we allow fear to stop us, then this quest is already failed."

Celestia clutched Bridgot's hand tightly in hers, running the fingers of her other hand across it, memorizing its design. She took a breath, stopping her tears and looking into his eyes, "Failure is not an option."

Celestia was awakened by Thaandor, and, as she groggily opened her eyes, she could see it was not yet dawn. "What is it?" she asked, sitting up.

"Stay quiet," he whispered, "Arm yourself."

She looked over at Bridgot, who had just been awakened by Kgansten, and the two of them grabbed their weapons. She seized her bow and quiver, notching an arrow. Looking around the dark, foggy woods, she couldn't see anything. The four of them backed toward each other, so they could each watch a different direction. Bridgot held up his sword, Kgansten raised his axe, Thaandor gripped his staff, and Celestia drew her bow.

"Get to the ferry!" Thaandor yelled suddenly.

They hurried to gather their things, getting the horses ready at top speed. Thaandor created a magical barrier as they did so, to protect them while they loaded their supplies. Once they were ready, they leaped upon their horses, riding for the ferry.

Behind them, Celestia caught a glimpse of dark faces coming after them through the shadowy forest. They rode hard, leaping upon the abandoned ferry. The ferrymen worked dawn to dusk, so there was no one there to ferry them across.

"Quickly!" Thaandor yelled, leaping from Chevron's back and untying the ferry.

Bridgot and Kgansten followed suit, as Celestia tried to keep the horses calm. She looked into the trees, just in time to see several gray-skinned men with fanged teeth, claws, and pointy ears on top of their heads running toward them, weapons in hand.

"Guys? What are those things?" she said, pointing.

"Get back!" Thaandor yelled, shoving Bridgot and Kgansten out of the way. With no ferry pole, Celestia didn't know how he intended to get them across the river. He raised his staff, bringing it down upon the ferry. It started moving across the river, just as the creatures reached the water's edge. A couple of them jumped onto the ferry before they got far enough away. Bridgot and Kgansten dispatched them quickly, dumping their bodies into the river. The ones on the shore screeched and hissed, waving their swords after them.

"What are those things?" Celestia asked again.

"Kodrizans," Thaandor said, "Servants of dark wizards. They are created through dark magic and ritual sacrifice to serve their master until death."

As he was giving his explanation, Celestia watched with horror as the kodrizans fired black arrows into the night sky. With what little light they had, she could just make out their outline, as the mass of arrows began to fall, directly toward the ferry.

Reacting quickly, she pulled out her wand, waving it over them. The shimmering blue wall of her shield formed over them as the arrows rained down upon it instead of them. The dark night was illuminated as Celestia glowed blue with magic. Her warriors stared at her in awe, watching the black arrows drop harmlessly into the river around them. The kodrizans reacted in terror to Celestia's power, scrambling over themselves to run away, back into the trees.

"Yes!" Bridgot yelled, "You go, honey!"

When the ferry reached the other side, they all got off, Celestia releasing her hold on the shield, and Thaandor sending the ferry back across the river for the ferryman. They moved through the forest as dawn crept through the trees, reaching the hill before Khanjgi.

"Let us catch up on our rest here," Thaandor said, "and we will work out a plan once we've recovered our strength."

They nodded their agreement, Kgansten taking the first watch as the rest of them settled down to catch up on sleep.

Around lunchtime, they all awoke, gathering around to eat and discuss the plan.

"The city of Khanjgi sits quietly ahead," Thaandor said, "I see no reason to think we'd be in danger waltzing right up to it."

"And if there is danger," Kgansten said, "we'll be walking right into a trap. We can't afford to risk it. We don't have the time. I say we ride the barrels inside, like the last time."

"I second that," Bridgot said, "It's too risky. If they are enemies, and they catch us, we'll never complete this quest in time. Our best chance is to sneak inside."

"What say you?" Thaandor asked, turning toward Celestia.

She paused, contemplating, "I say . . . we take the barrels in, just to be safe."

"Very well," Thaandor said, "So it shall be. Just before dawn tomorrow, we shall ride the barrels into the city."

They all nodded their agreement, spending the rest of the day relaxing, and keeping a watchful eye on the forest around them. Celestia spent her time lost in her thoughts, staring over the hill at the city of Khanjgi. It was a fortress, with dark gates, and a towering, black castle. She got chills, remembering the last time she'd sat looking at the ominous city. Last time, it marked the end of their quest. This time, it wasn't even close to over. That's what scared her the most.

"Strange, isn't it?" Bridgot asked, sitting beside her.

"What?"

"Being here again, all these years later, and it feels like nothing's changed," he answered, looking off at the city.

"Something like that," she agreed.

He was silent.

She realized he was feeling the same way as her. With all the pressure of being the "princess of the prophecy," she hadn't thought of the pressure her warriors faced. They were duty-bound to this quest as much as she was. They felt the same fear and worry. She set aside her own cares for a moment, grasping his hand, "Why don't we call our kids?"

He looked at her, "What?"

"We should talk to them before tomorrow. It may be our last chance."

He nodded.

She grabbed a bowl from the saddlebags, setting it in front of them and saying, "*Dwervo.*" The bowl filled with water, and she waited for it to settle before she called up her mother on the witch's glass.

"Celestia?" her mother said, appearing on the surface of the water.

"Hello, mother," she answered.

Bridgot waved, adding, "Hi, Eva."

"Hello, Bridgot," she replied, looking from him to her daughter, "It's been a while since you've called. What's happened?"

"We're in Khanjgi now," Celestia said, "We're trying to complete the prophecy still. We got what we needed from the wizards, and half of what we needed from the dragon riders. We have something to collect here, and then we must journey to the lands of the dwarves and the elves."

"I hadn't realized how long this would take," came her response, "I hope you find what you're looking for. Be careful, my child. Even I know Khanjgi is a dangerous place."

"How are you guys doing?" she asked.

"The war has spread," she said, "It's coming here. We won't be safe much longer. I'll have to take the children and go into hiding."

Bridgot and Celestia shared a look of worry. "I trust you to keep them safe," Celestia said, "Once we complete our quest, the war will end. You must only make it 'til then."

Lady Eva sighed, "Do what you must."

Celestia paused again, "May we speak to them?"

"Of course," her mother said solemnly, heading to the playroom. When she entered, Celestia could hear the playful laughter of her children, and she smiled to herself.

"Your mother and father would like to talk with the two of you," Eva said, handing the witch's glass to Prince Aurano.

As their children's faces appeared on the water, Bridgot and Celestia smiled. "Hello, my darlings," Celestia said.

"Mom! Dad!" Aurano yelled.

"Mommy! Daddy!" came Nastazya's voice as she jumped up and down, trying to reach her brother's height.

"Are you two being good?" Bridgot asked.

"Yes!" Nastazya shouted.

"How are you guys?" Aurano asked.

"We're just fine, angel," Celestia said, "We just wanted to see your bright, smiling faces. We'll be home when we can."

"How are your lessons coming?" Bridgot asked, obviously trying not to think about the fact that they might not make it back. Celestia squeezed his hand.

"Good," Nastazya shouted, "I got gold stars all week!"

"Excellent!" Bridgot said, "What about you, Aurano?"

"I'm doing fine," he said dryly, "Grandma says I know more kingdom history than she does."

Bridgot chuckled, "That's good to hear, son."

"How much longer will you be gone?"

"It might be a while, honey," Celestia chimed in, "But, don't worry. Everything will be fine. You'll see."

Aurano nodded, but their son was smart for his age. She could see that he knew the truth deep down. Nastazya was dancing around in the background, waving her bear in the air. It warmed Celestia's heart, seeing the sweet, naive innocence of their daughter.

"We love you guys," Bridgot said, "Don't ever forget it."

"I love you, too," Aurano said, handing the glass back to his grandmother.

"I love you, mommy! Love you, daddy!" Nastazya's voice rang out.

As her mother's face reappeared on the water, Celestia said, "We'll call again when we can. I love you, mom."

"I love you, too, darling," she said.

As she readied herself to sever the connection, she said, "Mom, wait."

"Yes, dear?"

"Before we go, could you take the witch's glass to Natasha and the boys?"

Lady Eva looked surprised for a moment, before she said, "Certainly." As she ventured down the corridor to the guest room where Kgansten's family was staying, Celestia turned to where Kgansten and Thaandor were relaxing.

"Kgansten," she called, "could you come over here a moment?"

He looked up with an expression of curiosity on his face. After a pause, he got up, coming over beside Celestia and Bridgot.

She saw Natasha's face appear on the water, and she waited until Kgansten noticed, "We'll give you a moment." She and Bridgot respectfully bowed out, allowing Kgansten to talk to his wife and kids.

When he was finished, Celestia severed the connection, watching Natasha's face disappear from the water's surface.

"Thank you," Kgansten said, giving them each a pat on the arm.

Celestia could see the gratitude in his eyes, and she realized that thinking of her warriors was rewarding by its own right. He needed to talk to his family as much as she and Bridgot did before venturing into Khanjgi. In spite of their bleak situation, she smiled. Even if they didn't make it, at least they got to talk to their loved ones one last time.

Just before dawn crept over the forest, the four of them slipped through the bushes to where the barrels lay. They left their horses at their campsite, as they would be unable to take them in the barrels with them.

"Watch out for Samson, Gjabreel, and Chevron, okay girl?" Celestia whispered to Razel, stroking her mane.

Razel whinnied, shaking her head.

"Good girl," she said, smiling.

She turned and followed the boys through the brush. They moved around to the barrels and saw a sight that left them all gawking. The massive skeleton of Ezmyra was still there, resting upon the hill beside the two graves they'd dug for Nastazya and Aurano. The flowers had long since died and blown away, but they could still make out the mounds of dirt.

"Bless me," Thaandor said breathlessly.

As Kgansten removed his helmet and Bridgot bowed his head respectfully, Celestia raised her wand. Feeling her powers coursing through her, she closed her eyes, visualizing two beautiful floral wreaths upon the graves. When she opened them, the flowers had appeared, just as she'd wished. She understood now how magic was rooted in emotion. Strong emotion evoked stronger powers than normal. Fear, rage, grief . . . they all helped her tap into her raw power. With it, she didn't need spells, just as Thaandor had said. She needed only her intent.

She turned toward her warriors, "Let's go."

They nodded, turning toward the barrels. Just then, they heard a rustling in the brush. As they stopped in their tracks, turning toward the sound, Celestia saw several faeries emerge. Her mouth opened in shock, as she realized they were still there, lurking in the forest beside Khanjgi.

"Into the barrels!" she shouted.

Kgansten clambered into the first one as Bridgot leapt into the second. Thaandor raised his staff to aid Celestia as the faeries smiled their evil grins. Their inky eyes and fanged teeth showed. They were just as dark and deadly as she remembered. One of them threw its blue magic directly at Celestia, and she dove out of the way as Thaandor blocked it with his wizard's shield. They began their attack, blasting them with their dark magic.

For a moment, Celestia was paralyzed by fear, unable to fight back. The recollection of how they'd killed Nastazya and Ezmyra was too much for her. Then, one of them launched their magic at Ezmyra's skeleton, blasting through her ribs. And, just like that, she was blinded by pure rage. Fear disappeared from her mind as she stood up, glowing blue with power, and blasting the horde of faeries back, through the trees.

They came back, trying to cast more attacks their way, but Celestia threw up her barrier, and none of their attacks got through. Thaandor gawked a moment, before jumping into the third barrel to wait. She focused her energy, feeling her powers fill her up, and the faeries converged on her, seeing it as a moment of weakness. As they swarmed around her, she opened her glowing eyes, smiling. They exchanged glances with one another, unsure.

With a mighty blast, she stood, releasing her powers around her. The faeries were thrown through the trees with terrified shrieks. Once the area was clear, Celestia pulled the lever, releasing the barrels, and jumping into the fourth one as they took off downstream toward the city.

She released her hold on her powers, watching the blue sparks fade from around her. They ducked down into the barrels as they passed through the opening into the city. They bumped into the cargo hold at the bottom, stopping their momentum.

They waited for voices, but heard none. After a few minutes, Celestia peered out of the top of her barrel. No one was around in the gloomy city. She climbed out of her barrel, leaping onto the dock. "Psst," she whispered, "Coast is clear. Come on."

Her three warriors climbed out of their barrels slowly, grouping up with her. They peered around the corner and saw no one in the town. There weren't even the usual travelers and salespeople in the marketplace. No one was there. They looked at each other.

Finally, Thaandor pushed through them, "Come on. But, move quickly and quietly."

They followed him around the corner, sticking close together, and moving like whispers through the abandoned city. As they peered into the surrounding buildings, they could see no one inside. The whole city was abandoned. Celestia had a growing ominous feeling as they walked. "It's just like Mashang," she whispered to Bridgot.

He nodded, looking as perturbed as she felt.

They made it to the castle with ease, venturing through the front gate. No guards were there to greet them.

"This way," Bridgot said, leading them up the stairs, and straight to the room in which Nazirdok had conducted his ritual. It was exactly how Celestia remembered it, as if it had remained untouched since that day. The table still lay on the floor, with the ritual objects scattered all around. The heavy feeling of dark magic hung in the air, and through the skylight, she could see the row of four remaining stars, still overhead, as it started to grow dark.

Celestia neared the table, feeling the pull of the object they would need to destroy. She bent down as her warriors watched, reaching out for a small crystal ball.

"Stop!" Thaandor yelled, rushing over and wrapping the ball in a cloth, "You must not touch it, else his powers could transfer into you."

"Wouldn't that be a pity?" a gravelly voice said suddenly.

They turned to see a young man step out from the shadowy corner of the room. He had brown hair and dark eyes. His skin had a grayish tint, and Celestia recognized the presence of evil within him.

"Who are you?" she demanded, stepping in front of her warriors.

He grinned, and she felt dark magic being summoned to him. She braced herself, tuning into her own current of power.

"I am Nazirdok's heir," he said, eyes turning black as night.

Zandor

7

"What do you mean, Nazirdok's heir?" Celestia asked.

He laughed humorlessly, "Well, I'm not his son if that's what you mean. I'm his apprentice. At least, I was. When you killed him, I was too young to fight. Now, I'm old enough to destroy you for what you did. That orb will be mine. I shall inherit his powers and take up his mission. I'll be more powerful than he ever was. And, unlike him, I won't let some powerless princess defeat me!"

As he spoke, his powers coalesced, and he let out a blast of dark energy, right toward them. Celestia threw up her barrier quickly, blocking his attack. When he saw her glowing blue, he gasped, eyes widening, "You know, I used to think I was the only one. This fight may prove more interesting than I thought."

It was Celestia's turn for her eyes to widen as she realized what he was saying, "You . . . you can tap into your raw powers, too?"

He grinned again, "Is that what you call it? I like it; it has a nice ring. Raw power." He looked down at his hands as the black sparks of dark magic cast shadows over his skin. After a pause, he looked back at her, sending another wave of power toward her.

Her warriors rushed from the room, taking the orb with them, as the magic collided with her shield, pushing her back. She looked back at him, feeling a drain of power for the first time since discovering she could wield her raw powers. He saw his opportunity and blasted her again. This time, it shattered her shield, throwing her across the room.

Thaandor appeared in the doorway, casting a spell at the dark wizard quickly. He wasn't expecting an outside attack, and the spell knocked him down. Thaandor seized the opportunity, pulling Celestia from the room and running. She clung to him as they ran, disoriented, ears ringing.

When they made it out of the castle, they rushed to catch up with Bridgot and Kgansten. As they ran through the city, an arm reached out of a doorway, grabbing Bridgot and pulling him inside. Kgansten charged in after him, and Thaandor led Celestia over to it.

Once they were all inside, the door was closed behind them, and they were being shoved through a trap door in the floor. They could hear the dark wizard storm past, his battle cries audible even underground. Celestia felt his energy, and she calmed her own, so he wouldn't pick up on it. Once he was past, they all breathed a sigh of relief. Looking around, they could see they were in a small, stone room, full of people.

"Who are all of you?" she asked, "Are you the townspeople?"

The sea of terrified faces looked back at her, unanswering. Finally, the woman who had pulled them in stepped forward. She had red hair and brown eyes, and wore a peasant's dress. "Yes," she said, "We belonged to this city. Now, we belong to no one."

A man—presumably her husband—stepped up beside her. He had blonde hair and brown eyes, "The armies of Mashang invaded. They slaughtered half the town. The rest of us went into hiding. When the armies moved south, we thought it was safe to come out, but then the dark wizard showed up. He took up the torch of Nazirdok and took over the castle."

"He tried to force us to follow him," the woman added, "But, we refused. He killed many more of us for our resistance. We've been trapped here ever since."

They looked around at the group of people again. They looked terrified, worn, and hungry. "How long have you been here?" she asked.

"Nearly two months," the man replied.

Celestia turned to her warriors, "That explains why no one was here, or in Mashang."

"This is far worse than I feared," Thaandor said.

"How do we get out of the city?" Bridgot asked.

There was nervous muttering throughout the group before the woman said, "No one has come or gone since the war with Mashang."

"What?" Kgansten cried, "You mean we're stuck here?"

"For the time being," Thaandor said, "It looks that way."

"But, you defeated Nazirdok," the man said, "You're heroes. Surely you can find a way out, or defeat *this* dark wizard."

"You know who we are?" Bridgot asked.

The people nodded.

"We recognized you when we saw you enter the town," the woman said.

"We thought you would defeat the dark wizard and save us all . . . again," the man added.

Celestia looked around at the hopeful faces, "I'm sorry. I'm afraid he's too strong. He has far more power than that of Nazirdok. And, unlike Nazirdok, he's prepared to face us. Our best chance is to fulfill The Great Prophecy and destroy the powers of Nazirdok. It will end this war, and the world will know peace." She turned to her warriors, "We have to get out of here. We still need three more weapons and one more warrior to destroy his remaining powers."

"Nazirdok is dead," the man said, "You killed him."

"Yes," Celestia agreed, "But his powers linger. They weren't completely destroyed. They are the cause of all this darkness. The dark wizard is his apprentice. He seeks to take on Nazirdok's powers, and his mission."

Sounds of panic spread quickly through the crowd.

"Everyone, remain calm," Thaandor said, "We got into the city easily enough. The dark wizard has already passed us, and is back in the castle by now. We shall simply walk out of the city."

Nervous whispers continued through the assembled group.

"Thaandor's right," Celestia agreed, "We can't stay holed up in here. We need to keep moving if we are to succeed."

"We're with you, lassie," Kgansten said.

Celestia *shushed* everyone, as she felt his energy outside again. It wasn't as strong now. She could tell he had released his hold on his raw powers. He went past the house again, toward the castle. She sighed once more, letting everyone know they were in the clear.

They waited a while longer to ensure he had gone back to the castle, and then they crept up the ladder into the house. They peered through the windows, looking around the empty city. No one was in sight. They waved for the townspeople to follow as they crept outside. Venturing through the city, they made their way to the front gate. It was a long, nerve-wracking walk, but they made it. Celestia and Thaandor went through, but, as the rest of the people tried to follow them, they were blocked by a magical barrier.

"It appears the gate has been charmed to only allow those with magical blood through," Thaandor said.

Celestia looked at Bridgot, panicking. He lifted the cloth containing the orb, handing it to her through the gate. She took it, and passed it to Thaandor, saying, "Go, get the horses!"

He scooped it out of her hands carefully, tightening the cloth around it, and running up the hill toward the horses.

As she heard the yells of the dark wizard erupt from the castle, she knew he could sense the barrier he'd put up, and whether anyone had gone through it. She focused in on her powers, and her will to save Bridgot. When the blue magic erupted around her, she walked forward, touching the gate. The barrier shattered, and the people ran through, fleeing east toward the parts of Kogatsa they knew were safe.

Once everyone was out, she waved her wand over the gate, creating a new barrier. This one would only allow those with *non*-magical blood through. She knew it wouldn't contain him forever, but she hoped it would buy them time. Time was the one thing they never had enough of. Thaandor arrived with the horses, and they leapt upon their backs, galloping south toward Kuttub. They got far enough away from Khanjgi that the dark wizard wouldn't likely find them in the night. Just to be safe, Thaandor put enchantments around their campsite, which would hide them from any unfriendly eyes.

As Celestia released her magic, she collapsed.

"Celestia!" Bridgot yelled, rushing to her side.

"She needs rest," Thaandor said, "Perhaps there *are* limits to raw power after all."

"We must exercise extreme caution through this place," Thaandor said as they journeyed through the day, putting Khanjgi far behind them.

"Why's that?" Kgansten asked.

"Because," Thaandor replied, "the townspeople said the armies of Mashang went south. That means they're here in Kuttub, unless they were brave enough to venture as far south as the land of the dwarves."

"Let's hope not," Kgansten said, "But, my people are fearsome warriors. It would be woe to the enemy who dared march upon our tunnels."

"Let us hope you're right," he said, adding, "We shall redouble our training efforts, Celestia. You must learn to master your powers, so you can face the dark wizard if necessary."

"Why would I have to face him?" she asked wearily, still recovering from the effects of her magic use, "He's back in Khanjgi. We have the orb. Our quest is to destroy it. He sits upon the throne of an abandoned city. He's no threat to us anymore."

"You are naive and foolish to think so," Thaandor snapped, "He's a very real, and very unexpected threat. I have a feeling we've not seen the last of him."

Celestia felt a knot in her stomach, and she knew Thaandor was right. *How can I master my powers enough to best him?* she thought, *He's far stronger than me. How is it he was able to train so much more to use his raw power?*

They journeyed through the day in silence, sticking to the shadows. Bridgot stayed close to Celestia, watching her carefully. She smiled weakly at him, appreciating his concern. She was far more exhausted than she ever had been after using her powers before. When evening came, they made camp in a secluded area enclosed by some boulders.

"Let us work on your training," Thaandor said once they'd eaten their meal.

Celestia nodded, taking a breath.

"Tell me what you've discovered about your powers," he said, eyeing her, "You've been able to tap into them at will more easily. You've even cast spells without words."

She sighed, "I discovered the source of my strength. It's rooted in emotion. Strong emotions evoke strong magic. When I have that, I don't need a spell. It's just as you said—I need only my intent. But, when I don't have strong emotion related to a spell, it's useful to use incantations to direct my power."

"Hmm," he said, scratching his gray-bearded chin, "What of your energy?"

"I'm far more drained than normal," she replied, "I still feel tired, as though I haven't slept at all."

"I'm going to teach you a very complicated spell," he said, "Do you think you can handle it?"

She nodded.

"Okay, you'll need to tune into your current of power, and move it. We shall use your wedding ring. You will learn to store your energy reserves for later use. I should have taught you this before, but I didn't think you'd have need of it, with your ability to wield raw power. Focus on moving your power and your energy into the ring. When you're ready, use the incantation—"

"No," Bridgot said suddenly, "No spells tonight. Can't you see she's exhausted? I won't risk her over-exerting herself."

"It's alright, Bridgot," she said.

"No, it's not," he looked at her, going to her side, "It's not alright. You need rest. You can learn the spell tomorrow."

"Very well," Thaandor said, "Perhaps he's right. It is riskier to learn spells when you're tired. Let's all just . . . get some rest."

Bridgot let out a sigh of relief, "I'll take the first watch."

They moved through the next day quickly, covering a lot of ground. Celestia had recovered her strength, and she was grateful to Bridgot for preventing her from over-exerting herself. He smiled at her, and she could tell that he saw how much better she looked.

When they stopped to make camp that night, Thaandor said, "Do you feel ready tonight to learn the storing spell?"

"Yes," Celestia answered, "I'm ready."

"Very well," he continued, "Remember what I told you last night. Focus on moving your power into your ring. The incantation is *Carbonis*."

She tuned into her energy current—she was getting quite good at that. When she felt it strongly, she aimed her wand at her silver-banded wedding ring, saying, "*Carbonis*." She could feel her energy slowly draining from her. She watched in amazement as the blue powers highlighting her skin streamlined into the diamond atop her ring.

"When you feel tired, like you need sleep, release the spell," Thaandor was saying, "You don't want to go too far, or it could kill you."

Celestia began to feel her powers waning, no longer in their raw form, and, as she felt ready to sleep, she knew it was long enough, and she released the spell.

"Good," Thaandor said, "Do that every night, and soon your ring will house a great reserve of energy which you'll be able to use when you need it most."

She nodded, curling up on the ground to sleep as Thaandor took the first watch.

The next couple of days breezed by as they moved through Kuttub. There were no signs of life along the way, and they began to wonder just how far the destruction of the armies of Mashang had reached. Each night, as they camped, Celestia stored her energy in her ring, building her reserve. Bridgot stuck close to her, ready to defend her if need-be when her strength was low.

One night, when they stopped to make camp, she tapped into her raw powers, aiming her wand at the ring. "*Car—*" she began.

She was interrupted by a war cry, as a group of soldiers came down on their campsite.

Thaandor grabbed his staff, blasting them back. Bridgot and Kgansten took up sword and axe, readying themselves for a fight. Celestia stopped her spell, rising, powers glowing around her. The soldiers charged back in, faltering when they saw her. They looked at each other, and then continued their advance. Bridgot, Kgansten, and Thaandor fought them off as normal. Celestia stood there, staring with her glowing eyes at the oncoming soldiers.

When they charged her, she blasted them back as though they were nothing. After a few blasts, she grabbed a soldier by his throat, looking at him, directly into his soul, "Why do you continue your attack when you cannot hope to best my power?"

"I'm just . . . following orders," he choked out.

"Whose orders?" she demanded.

"Z-Zandor," he replied.

"Who?" she asked, pulling him closer.

"The dark wizard of Khanjgi—Nazirdok's heir."

"He sent you after us?"

"Y-Yes. He commands the armies of Mashang, Kogatsa, and now, Kuttub," he said, "He ordered us to ambush you."

"Why?" she demanded, "He knows you cannot beat me."

"To steal . . . the orb," he said, "Please . . . that's all I know."

She dropped him, and he took off running. She turned toward their campsite, ensuring the orb was safe. The cloth in which it had been wrapped was empty. A soldier had swiped it while they were distracted. She located him quickly, pulling out her wand. As he attempted to leap upon his horse and ride away, she directed her magic at him, knocking him down in mid-air. "*Goncor*," she said, aiming at the orb. It lifted from the ground beside the soldier, and she moved it with her magic, causing it to float back to the campsite, and be re-wrapped in its cloth.

Blast after blast and wave after wave, the soldiers kept coming. Celestia kept a careful eye upon the orb, blasting anyone who got too close. Now that she knew their mission, it was all too easy for her to keep them away from the orb. As the fight wore on, and the seemingly endless wave of soldiers continued to swarm them, Celestia's energy began to wane. Finally, she had to release her hold on her raw powers.

"Celestia?" Bridgot asked, positioning himself close to her, "Are you alright?"

"We have to get out of here," she said, "There's too many of them. They're after the orb."

He nodded, searching the landscape for a way out. "There's a cliff, not too far," he said, as he continued to swing his sword, cutting down any soldiers that approached, "When we passed it earlier, I heard water at the bottom. There's a little trail close by that the horses could use, but if the soldiers were to follow us, they'd reach us in the river below."

"Send Kgansten and Thaandor with the horses," she said, "We'll distract them. Keep the orb with us. If that's what they're after, they won't pay attention to them."

He nodded, moving over to the other two and telling them the plan. They loaded up the horses quickly, fighting all the while. Bridgot tucked the orb into his cape, moving back to Celestia's side. Kgansten and Thaandor led the horses away, off to the trail that would lead them to the bottom of the cliff.

In the meantime, Celestia had pulled out her sword to fight. She was right, and none of the soldiers paid any attention to Kgansten, Thaandor, and the horses, focusing instead on the orb in Bridgot's possession. The two of them fought side-by-side, getting pushed back by the sheer number of soldiers. They started moving toward the cliff, backing away as they fought. The soldiers pursued them, believing they had the upper hand.

When they had backed up as far as they could, and their feet were dancing with the edge of the cliff, the soldiers smiled. "Hand over the orb," one of them said, "and we'll let you live."

"As generous an offer as that is," Bridgot replied, "I think we're gonna have to pass." With that, he grabbed Celestia, jumping off the cliff. The soldiers clustered at the edge, looking down after them. Thaandor broke their fall with magic as they landed in a boat.

They could hear the yells of the soldiers as they tried to figure out how to pursue them. "Hurry," Celestia said, "We must get away from here as quickly as possible, before they can find a place to catch up with us."

"I know," Thaandor said, using his powers to propel the boat.

"Exactly how did you find a boat?" Bridgot asked.

"Well, this nice fisherman we ran into lent it to us," he answered.

"Well," Kgansten inserted, "Lent it to us against his will."

Celestia and Bridgot followed Kgansten's gaze to a man with black hair and brown eyes, sitting at the back of the boat, who was tied to the stern, with a cloth tied around his mouth.

"What are you doing?" she asked in astonishment.

"Getting us out of here," Thaandor replied.

"Don't worry," Kgansten said, "We'll let him go, and return his boat, as soon as we're safely away from here."

"Sorry about this, sir," Celestia said to the fisherman, "We're really not bad people. This was an emergency."

"Why don't you rest," Bridgot said worriedly, "I can tell that the battle took its toll on you."

"I'll rest later," she brushed him off, "Right now, I have questions. Thaandor."

He looked at her.

"If he's powerful enough to command the armies of three countries, and he's after the orb, how are we to keep it safe until we can destroy it?"

"His armies won't get past the armies of the dwarves," he answered, "Once we reach Korga, we'll be safe."

"Didn't you say you think I'll have to face him again before this is over?"

"Yes," he said, "I'm not sure how everything will play out, but we have to gather the remaining weapons and warrior, and destroy the orb before it's too late. What *I'm* trying to work out is: why did he not touch the orb before we got there? It hadn't moved since you destroyed Nazirdok. The people had been in hiding nearly two months. He was in the room already when we got there. Who knows how long he'd been in the castle. Either he didn't know the orb was there before, he didn't know which object it was, or he didn't know that it existed and what it could do."

"It doesn't matter," Celestia said, "What matters is that he *didn't* touch it, and we still have a chance. We narrowly avoided the virtual return of Nazirdok. Now, we must avoid the undoing of the prophecy."

Korga

8

They remained on the water the next couple of days, speeding up their journey through Kuttub. The current of the water propelled them forward, and they were able to take turns steering during their shifts at night. With the constant movement, they were able to cover far more ground than they would have been able to by horseback.

The fisherman was untied and allowed to eat and use the bathroom. He was obviously unhappy with the situation, but he didn't dare to say anything or try to attack them. Celestia could tell he was afraid to. He remained silent, waiting for the return of his boat.

They sailed all the way to the border of Korga, climbing off the boat and bidding farewell to the fisherman. He angrily turned the boat around, muttering curses at them and sailing away as quickly as he could before they could change their minds. Celestia chuckled to herself, shaking her head. She felt the sensation of her body still being on the boat, despite the fact they were back on land, and she had a tough time climbing upon Razel's back.

The four of them rode their horses right up to the massive doors that marked the entrance to the dwarven tunnels, going inside. The guards to the entrance bowed at the sight of Kgansten, allowing them to pass.

"It seems you command a great deal of respect, Kgansten," Celestia said.

"Well," he said, blushing, "I *am* a Dwarf Lord, now."

"Still," she continued, "I don't believe Lord Dingus commanded the same respect."

"Of course not," Lord Kgansten said, "He was a swine."

Celestia chuckled, and then turned serious, "You're a good man, Kgansten."

"Thank you, milady," he said, bowing his head as he rode upon his spotted pony.

They journeyed through the dark tunnels of the dwarves, and Celestia remembered how much she had missed the sunlight the first time she'd journeyed through. Still, the tunnel system built by the dwarves was no less impressive. The whole place was carved into intricate designs, with jewels embedded within them. It was a masterpiece of craftsmanship which she had never seen the equivalent of. Though the lantern-light could not compare to the sun in this underground world, she felt safer here than out in the human realm, where the armies of Zandor were preparing a war against her and her warriors.

It would take them a fortnight to reach the kingdom of Dirthix, where the Dwarven Hall of Weapons was located. Celestia could feel that the dwarven weapon they needed was there. Her senses had been heightened by her newfound powers, and she couldn't believe what she was able to sense, now. Nothing was a surprise anymore, except for Zandor. She guessed she couldn't sense him before due to his ability to wield raw powers as well. There was a lot she didn't yet understand about raw power. It would be a journey in and of itself to explore her new ability.

As they continued through the tunnels, Thaandor continued to train her, working with her each night, and teaching her new spells. He showed her how to access her energy stores when she needed to use them, how to magically store objects, and how to counter an energy blast. Magical combat piqued her interest most of all, naturally, since it was the most useful thing she could currently learn. She knew she would have to face Zandor before this was over, and she wanted to be prepared for it.

There were many different kinds of energy blasts. They each had different effects. Some were intended to kill, some to maim, some to simply knock back. Some of them were good for blocking, some for breaking another wizard's shield, some for pushing them backward. She had to try to master them all before facing Zandor again. Though emotion would help, it wouldn't be enough to simply cast aimless attacks at him. She would need some guidance for her powers.

How much was Nazirdok able to teach him? she wondered. Without knowing exactly what she was up against, she had to be prepared for anything.

A little over a week went by, and they reached Kgansten's territory. Celestia remembered when it had been the territory of Lord Dingus, and they had feared to cross through. The battle they'd had, which had made Kgansten and Aurano friends after Aurano saved his life, came back to her like it was yesterday. She almost let out a laugh, thinking of how they had once been afraid of the likes of Lord Dingus. Now, someone of his stature was the least of their concerns.

"Welcome to my domain," Kgansten said grandly, "It feels good to be home. Though we're still on this quest, it's like taking a much-needed break."

They followed him to his dwarven mansion, finally able to rest in beds for a change. Celestia hadn't yet been to his house, and she was blown away once again by the sheer size of the structures the dwarves built. She never understood why such small people created such large structures. It was a sprawling manor, crafted from glittering stones. It had several tall towers and a massive front door. Kgansten led them to his stable, where they set up the horses for the night.

They went inside, and it resembled the tunnels, with intricate carvings and sparkling gems. It was gorgeous, and Celestia marveled at the mosaics of Kgansten's family history. Tales of warriors, romance, and joyous celebrations adorned his walls and ceiling.

"It's breathtaking," Celestia said.

"Yes," Kgansten agreed, "I think so each time I see it. It never gets old, even when you live here."

She smiled.

"Right this way to the guest rooms," he said.

He led them up a grand, golden staircase, and down a hall to a couple of rooms. They reminded her of the massive suites King Thanghor had given them when they'd stayed in his kingdom. They, too, were adorned with beautiful dwarven artwork. The beds were huge, and she knew they were in for a night of well-earned sleep.

"So, this is home for you, huh?" Celestia asked.

"Indeed it is," Kgansten said, "Though, I must admit it doesn't feel like home right now."

"Because we're still on this quest?" Bridgot asked.

"Because my family's not here," he replied.

Bridgot looked at him in surprise, and then looked down sadly.

"Home is where your family is," Kgansten said.

Bridgot patted his arm, sharing a look of understanding.

"Well, everyone get some rest," Kgansten said, "Tomorrow, we shall set out for Dirthix. We have only a few more days before we reach it."

"Goodnight, Kgansten," Celestia said, heading into the guest room she and Bridgot were to share.

Bridgot followed, and Thaandor went into the guest room across the hall. Kgansten headed to his own room, and Celestia thought she had never seen him look so down. The proud Dwarf Lord was a family man at heart, and it was true what he had told her that night: he loved his wife and kids. She could see how much he missed them, and she knew they had to complete this quest so he could see them again. As she thought of that, she thought of her own children, and how much she missed them. She and Bridgot had their own family to fight for.

This quest wasn't about anyone, and yet, it was about everyone. As she drifted off to sleep that night, she let thoughts of everything she had to fight for drift through her mind. Before she faded completely out of consciousness, she felt Bridgot's lips against her forehead, and she thought she heard him whisper, "I love you."

When morning came, it was time to set out again. They pulled their steeds from the stable, setting out through the tunnels once more, the *click-clack* of their hooves hitting the marble floor as they rode. The tunnels began to look more and more familiar the closer they got to Dirthix. Celestia learned more and more about magic as they traveled, learning spells for combat, as well as for other useful purposes to their travels, such as producing food and repairing clothing. Spells were more powerful when she tapped into her raw power, but it wasn't always necessary. Some spells were simple enough to not require full use of her strength.

The energy store in her ring grew each day, and she knew by using her raw power to fill it, it had far greater reserves than the average wizard could accomplish. She could only hope that Zandor hadn't discovered this particular secret of Nazirdok's. If he had, she still had no hope of beating him. Though, with the right combination of spells, she thought she might be able to, if his training hadn't advanced as far.

These thoughts and more filled her mind each day, and made it hard for her to sleep at night. Luckily, the power drain before bed wore her out enough that her mind could little resist her body's need for rest. Though it put her at risk if they were to be attacked in the night, she trusted her husband to protect her if need be. Any foes they faced in these tunnels would be insignificant in comparison to the ones they'd already faced. Her warriors could handle a siladine or a rogue Dwarf Lord easily.

It took only a few days to reach the kingdom of Dirthix. It was just as grand as Celestia remembered, and they went straight to the palace of King Thanghor, to request permission to borrow the required dwarven weapon. His throne room was massive, golden, and full of jewels and gold. He sat upon his golden throne, garbed in a too-tall crown and a too-long cape, with a blonde beard.

"Welcome, friends!" he said, "And, welcome home, Kgansten. You've been away quite a while. We thought you'd gotten lost!"

"No," Kgansten replied, "I only embarked upon a quest."

"A quest? Really?" he said, "It's been a while since you've done anything of the sort."

"Yes," he agreed, "Not since the last time I went with these two."

"An honor, as always," King Thanghor said, bowing his head to Queen Celestia and King Bridgot. "Where's the family?" he asked, turning back to Kgansten.

Kgansten grimaced, looking pained, "They're still in Duwazo. I thought it would be safer for them in one place, rather than to make the journey without me. You see, war has broken out across the land. They are safe with Queen Celestia's mother and children. I wish they were here, in the dwarven tunnels. But, the journey through Gachichken is too risky. It's better they stay where they are."

"War?" he said, looking surprised, "What war?"

"You stay blind to the world here in these tunnels, Uncle Thanghor," he said, "Kingdoms of Duwazo are at war with each other. The northwest corner of Gachichken is at war with Cardeas. And, a dark wizard in Khanjgi commands the armies of Kogatsa, Mashang, and Kuttub. He seeks to fulfill Nazirdok's mission, and prevent us from completing the prophecy. You see, though we killed Nazirdok, his powers were not destroyed. They linger, and, until we can destroy them, evil will spread, infecting all lands of this world like a disease."

King Thanghor's eyes widened, and he grew pale as his nephew spoke.

"We have only until the last of the stars that aligned falls to fulfill our quest. We come seeking a dwarven weapon with which we can destroy Nazirdok's powers."

He didn't say anything, still looking perturbed.

"You should send the dwarven armies to the tunnel entrances, to ensure our people's safety. Please, uncle, may we have your permission to borrow one of the dwarven weapons from the Hall of Weapons, which Queen Celestia will identify?" Kgansten pleaded.

"You may have anything you need, nephew," he answered, "You know this."

"Thank you, uncle," he said.

King Thanghor nodded, still looking pale. Celestia could see he was in shock, but they had no time to waste. He had given them his full permission. All they had to do now was to find the weapon and take it.

"Yes, thank you, sir," she said, ushering her warriors out of the throne room. Once they were back in the hallway, she turned to look at them, "Lead the way, Kgansten. Let's get to this Hall of Weapons."

He nodded, looking disheartened.

"Give him time to process everything," Celestia said, "Your uncle will be alright. He's a good man, and a good king. He wouldn't lead your people astray."

"We'll finish this quest before the armies ever reach these tunnels," Bridgot added.

Kgansten nodded again, his expression the same. He led them down a long corridor, and into a structure as large as the palace. "Welcome to the Dwarven Hall of Weapons," he said, "Celestia, I leave the rest to you."

She nodded, making a beeline through the Hall. She knew exactly where the weapon was. Her internal compass had been pulling her there since the moment they'd entered the tunnels. It was an axe, housed in a glass display case rimmed with gold. The axe was beautifully crafted, with jewels embedded throughout the handle as well as the bit.

"This is it," she said.

Kgansten stood gawking, open-mouthed.

"What is it?" she asked.

"This is the axe of Kgoresh the Terrible. He's the most famous dwarven warrior in history!" he answered, staring at it in awe. "To think a common Dwarf Lord like me will have the privilege of wielding it. . ."

"I'm afraid I don't know much dwarf history," Celestia said, "But, the weapons we've gathered so far have been very special, so I can only assume this one is, too."

He nodded, "You have no idea, lassie." He turned toward the guards, "By order of Lord Kgansten, and with special permission from King Thanghor, remove this weapon from its case."

"Sir?" one of them asked.

"This is the axe of Kgoresh the Terrible," the other said.

Kgansten stared at them for a moment, giving them a look that said *and?* When they didn't move, he said, "Am I to understand that you will be defying the orders of your king?"

"No, sir," they said hurriedly, opening the case, and handing him the axe.

Kgansten grasped the handle, lifting it carefully, and with great reverence. He looked as though he'd never seen a more amazing sight.

Celestia gave him a moment before she said, "We should go. We must set out at dawn."

"You're *taking* the axe?" one of the guards asked.

Kgansten looked at him, "*Borrowing*. It shall be returned at the conclusion of our quest. King Thanghor thanks you for your cooperation."

They looked at each other uneasily as Kgansten tucked the axe into his belt.

Celestia and her warriors headed out of the Hall of Weapons, and Kgansten located Felix and Seamus, who led them to a few rooms for the night. They were the same rooms they'd stayed in on the first quest, and Celestia was relieved that this time around, she and Bridgot could share the suite. Before going to bed, they called her mother.

"Hello, darling," her mother answered.

"Hi, mom," she said, "We made it through Khanjgi, and got what we went in for. We're in the land of the dwarves, now. We got what we needed from them, thanks to Kgansten, and we're setting out at dawn for the land of the elves."

"That's wonderful, darling. I'm glad you're alright. How many more things do you need?"

"Just two more objects, and one more warrior," she replied, "How are things there?"

"Not good," her mother said, "The war has reached the kingdom."

It was then that Celestia realized her mother was whispering, "Where are you?"

"We're in the safe-house," Lady Eva replied, "Natasha and the boys are with us. We're all alive and well. The kids are handling the situation better than expected. They're just playing away. But, the army of Kiteau and their allies are infiltrating the kingdoms allied with Chemsson in order to systematically defeat them. We were next on the list. They've invaded the castle."

"What happened?" Celestia asked, panicked.

Bridgot squeezed her shoulder, pulling her close. She could tell he was worried, too.

"Well, when I heard them approaching the castle, one of the servants had just come to inform me. I rushed to the children's rooms and plucked them from their beds, grabbing a few of their belongings. I went to get Natasha and her sons, and I could hear them break down the door and storm inside. She got her kids ready quickly, and we rushed to the safe-house. The servants helped us escape, and they went to their families' homes within the kingdom for safety. We've been here since, waiting for the war to end."

"Let me see them," Celestia said, eyes widening.

Eva turned the witch's glass so Celestia could see Natasha and the five children.

She breathed a sigh of relief when she saw her son and daughter, playing with Kgansten's kids, perfectly safe and unharmed. "I'm so glad you're all alright," she said.

"Me, too," her mother replied, "Finish your quest with haste. We shall be waiting for you."

Celestia nodded, severing the connection. "Oh, Bridgot," she said, turning into him.

He held her close, not saying anything. She could feel his worry, but he just held her tightly, conveying it through touch. She wrapped her arms around him, taking comfort in his embrace.

Gliken

9

When dawn came, the four of them set out, departing the land of the dwarves and heading into the forest, toward the land of the elves. Celestia was relieved to exit the dwarven tunnels and breathe the fresh air in again. After a few weeks in the darkness, the sunlight was bright, but welcoming. A few dirthens flew past overhead, and burrowed into the ground beside the tunnels. Kgansten looked up at them dejectedly, bidding farewell to his homeland.

They ventured into the trees, and Celestia patted Razel's side. She knew the forest of the elves made the horses nervous. The trees slowly changed from brown and green to silvery and bluish. The feeling of ancient magic hung in the air, and she knew they had arrived in Gliken. She caught sight of the creatures of the elven forest: pixies, stags, dwervas, auristras, and even mermaids.

Then, out of the corner of her eye, she saw one of the rarest sights of all: a unicorn. The pure white, horse-like creature with the horn on top of its head stood just inside the treeline, watching them carefully. Celestia returned its stare in amazement, locking eyes with the incredible creature. She felt the pull of its magic on her own, and, as she was trying to figure out what it meant, there was a burst of light and a deafening explosion as a star fell near the creature, scaring it off.

"We're running out of time!" Thaandor yelled, "We must ride with haste to Garellis!"

They quickened their pace, covering a great deal of ground before nightfall. When they stopped to make camp, Thaandor said, "We should reach the kingdom of Garellis tomorrow evening. That's where we shall find the elven weapon, right, Celestia?"

"Yes," she answered, "I can feel it's there."

"Don't forget," Bridgot added, "We must also find a warrior. We cannot hope to complete this quest without one."

They all nodded solemnly.

"King Boreas is a reasonable man," Thaandor said, "Surely, he will help us."

"Kirstiana is a reasonable woman," Celestia retorted, "And yet, the council of the dragon riders did not see fit to grant us a warrior."

"Grief does things to people," Bridgot said, "I fear the elves will feel similarly to the dragon riders about extending us their aid."

Thaandor paused, "Get some rest, all of you. I'll take the first watch. The only way to find out their position is to ask. We won't know for certain until tomorrow."

They rode through the day, deeper into Gliken. When evening came, they reached the misty kingdom of Garellis. They recognized the elven citizens, milling slowly about, and the tree structures—the living city of the elves—brought into existence by magic. They ran into Thaddeus—the tall, dark general of the elven army—on their way into the city. He led them to the palace, taking their steeds and showing them inside, to the throne room of King Boreas.

The dark-skinned elf king sat upon his green, flowered throne, staring at them expectantly. He had dark eyes and long, black hair. His iridescent robes gave off shades of opal as he moved. "Welcome, friends," he said, "What brings you to the kingdom of Garellis?"

Thaandor explained the situation to him; how the prophecy wasn't fulfilled, and they needed a weapon and a warrior from the elves to destroy Nazirdok's powers.

King Boreas sat pondering for a moment. After a while, he said, "Locate the weapon you require and return here with it. I shall then decide if I will grant you my permission. Thaddeus will accompany you. He bears my seal of approval to bring the weapon before me. You may go in the morning. As for tonight, Marcos will show you to your rooms." He waved to his assistant, who stood, heading out of the throne room.

They all nodded, following Marcos down the hall to the rooms they'd been given on their previous quest. They had to open another one, so all four of them could have a room. Bridgot shared the one Celestia had been in before, and Kgansten took the one Bridgot had occupied. Marcos opened another room beside Kgansten's that Thaandor took.

It was just as magical as Celestia remembered. The bed made from moss and ferns was strange, but comfortable. The scents of the evening flowers gave the room a calming air. Through the window, which was an opening formed in the tree wall, they could see the lanterns and pixies, giving off their soft luminescence.

After washing up, she and Bridgot settled in to sleep, sinking into the plant life of the bed. It squeezed them softly, as though they were being cradled by Mother Earth herself. Soothing lavender wafted over her, and she breathed it in, drifting off peacefully.

Thaddeus came to get them in the morning. He led them to the Museum of Elven Weapons. It was another beautifully crafted tree structure, with twisting branches forming the walls and floor. Inside, there were halls full of famous elven weapons and artifacts. The cases were partially covered with moss and vines, leaving spaces to see the weapons within.

Celestia went straight to the required weapon, feeling it so closely within their grasp. It was along one of the walls, in an unpretentious case. It didn't appear to be a weapon of great significance to the elves, in comparison with some of the other weapons in their museum. "This one," she said, looking for the name of its owner. As Thaddeus stepped forward to remove it from its case, she found it. "Aurano," she whispered.

It was Aurano's bow and quiver. The others looked solemnly at it as Thaddeus led them back to the palace to get permission from King Boreas. The silvery elven bow and its arrows were so beautifully crafted. They missed its owner terribly, but Celestia couldn't say she was surprised that this was the weapon they needed from the elves.

When they re-entered the throne room, King Boreas looked surprised. "That didn't take long," he said, "Very well. Present the weapon."

Thaddeus handed it to him, saying, "The bow and quiver of Aurano."

He took it solemnly, looking it over, and looking back at them, "Do you intend to toy with the emotions of our race?"

"Of course not," Thaandor said.

"I can sense which weapons are needed, as he said," Celestia inserted, "It may seem a little too coincidental, but, it does seem fitting, don't you think?"

"How so?" he asked, unamused.

"The weapon required to complete our quest and fulfill the prophecy is the very weapon used by the warrior of our previous quest, to fulfill the same prophecy."

He paused, considering, "Very well. I shall grant you permission to borrow this weapon. But, it must be returned."

"Of course," she said, "It shall be."

"I cannot in good conscience grant you a warrior, however," he continued, "Last time, it didn't go so well."

"We understand your reasons," Bridgot said, "But, without an elven warrior, we cannot fulfill the prophecy. We cannot destroy his powers. Allowing us to borrow the weapon is pointless, with no one to wield it. You doom us to fail."

"Then, return the weapon," he countered.

"We shall accept your generous offer," Thaandor said quickly, "and borrow the weapon."

"Tonight, there will be a feast," he said, looking at them dubiously, "Rest and recover your strength. Tomorrow, you may set out at dawn to complete your quest."

Thaandor bowed in acceptance, heading out of the room, and waving for the remaining three to follow him. They went down the hall and back to their guest rooms.

Before they went inside, Bridgot turned on Thaandor, demanding, "Why did you do that?"

"He was obviously not going to budge," Thaandor responded, "I didn't want to lose the weapon while we were at it. That's one less thing to worry about."

"Well, now we have one *more* thing," Bridgot said, "We have no warrior to wield it."

"We must find another way," Thaandor replied, "This quest will not be doomed to fail."

The rest of the day, they took things slow, using the time to rest and relax, and preparing themselves to set out the following day. The feasting began around lunchtime, and they all took their seats, enjoying the elven delicacies. Kgansten looked miserable, trying to fill up on fruits and vegetables, when dwarves were used to meats and cheeses. Celestia didn't mind either way, and the crisp vegetables were quite filling with the various breads. The fruits were juicy and sweet, and full of flavor. They made up for the lack of substance, and she could see why the elves enjoyed them so.

While they were eating, a dark-skinned elven woman approached them, sitting beside Celestia. She didn't say anything, and they continued eating, unsure. Celestia exchanged glances with her warriors, and they all eyeballed the woman. She was an elven beauty, with long, flowing black hair, and hazel eyes. She wore grassy green elven robes, with a gold band adorning her head.

She leaned toward Celestia, whispering, "I want to help you. Meet me in the clearing through the trees to the left of the river after the feast."

With that, the mysterious woman got up, moving to another table inconspicuously. Her warriors all looked at her questioningly, obviously wanting to know what she'd whispered to her. She shook her head slightly, indicating she couldn't tell them there.

When the feast was over, they headed for the palace with several of the king's servants and warriors, and Celestia pulled her own warriors to the side, gesturing for them to follow her quietly. She hoped no one noticed as they snuck away from the group, ducking behind the winding staircases and large tree trunks. Celestia led them toward the river, and followed it left, into the trees.

They reached a clearing, and Bridgot said, "Will you tell us what's going on now?"

"She said she wanted to help us, and to meet her here after the feast," Celestia answered.

"You came," a voice said. The woman glided into the clearing, looking at them with her intense hazel eyes.

"You said you wanted to help us," Celestia replied.

She smiled, "Indeed."

"She's an elven witch. Don't fall for her tricks," Kgansten said, "She's lured us here under false pretenses."

"No, master dwarf," she said, "I'm not a witch. I'm an elven warrior-in-training."

Celestia smiled, "Warrior?"

"Why do you want to help us?" Bridgot asked.

"How did you even know of our quest?" Thaandor inserted.

"I am Princess Xharia, daughter of King Boreas," she said, "I overheard your conversation with my father. Unlike him, I'm prepared to help you. As for why, well . . . Aurano was my friend. We trained together, and he made me a better warrior. I heard what you said about his death meaning nothing if you fail. I can't let that happen. And besides, warriors-in-training are constantly looking for opportunities to become full-fledged warriors."

"So, you'd like to be our elven warrior?" Celestia said.

Xharia nodded.

"I don't trust it," Kgansten said stubbornly.

"We don't have much choice," Thaandor countered.

"She was friends with Aurano," Celestia said, "That's good enough for me."

"How come we never met you before?" Bridgot asked.

"My father likes to keep his family hidden from outsiders," Xharia replied, "He believes it keeps us safe. He doesn't know what a skilled fighter I am. He refuses to grant me an opportunity to prove myself. He thinks he knows what's best for me, and he wants to keep me out of harm's way. But, he doesn't see how he pushes me away by the very things he does for my protection."

Celestia smiled again, "You're in. We leave at dawn, south toward Katangalo, and the village of Kataran. If you really want to help us, get your horse and join us."

Though her warriors protested her decision, they all knew they had no choice. It was that or fail. So, they got their horses saddled and ready, riding toward Bridgot's village, where Celestia felt the presence of the human weapon. As they rode, the trees slowly faded back to green and brown, and the presence of magic dwindled away. They made it all the way out of Gliken before Xharia caught up with them.

"I was beginning to think you weren't coming," Celestia said.

"I couldn't be seen departing the forest of the elves with all of you," Xharia replied, "else I might've been caught and sent back."

"Wouldn't that be a shame," Kgansten grumbled.

"Easy, Seina," she said, patting her white stallion.

"Seina?" Celestia asked, looking at her horse.

"Yes," Xharia said, "Aurano's mother couldn't afford to keep him, but she didn't want him to go too far, so she gave him to me to care for."

"A likely story," Kgansten said, "You stole Aurano's horse, and now, you want to accompany us on the quest *he* started?"

"Is that why you dislike me so?" Xharia asked, "You feel as though I replaced Aurano on your quest?"

Kgansten's mouth opened and closed for a minute, before he looked away, crossing his arms as he rode.

"I could never replace him," she said softly, "He was a truly exceptional warrior, and friend. I only wish to ensure his memory is honored the way it should be . . . the way he deserves."

He looked back at her then, his expression softening, "As long as you know he can never be replaced."

Xharia nodded, "He was special to all of us." After a pause, she added, "I saw you cry at his funeral. You cared for him a great deal."

Kgansten looked away again, hiding his face.

"We may not have known him as long as you," Bridgot said, "But, he was our friend as much as yours. We all cared for him, the same as you."

She nodded again, "I know."

They rode in silence until they found a spot to make camp, setting up for the night. Bridgot took the first watch as they all settled in to sleep. Xharia gawked in wide-eyed amazement when Celestia stored her energy for the day in her ring. Celestia had never seen an elf impressed by the skills of a human before, even a witch. She giggled to herself as she drifted off to sleep.

Katangalo

10

A s the golden rays of the sun peeked over the horizon, they set out again. It only took until lunchtime to reach Kataran. When they did, several villagers spotted them riding in. Soon enough, the whole town came out to meet them.

"Bridgot's here!" they cheered.

His family rushed from their house to greet them, and, as they dismounted their horses, smothered him and Celestia in hugs and kisses. The elders came forward, silencing the crowd, "What business brings you here?" He eyed Kgansten, Thaandor, and Xharia meaningfully.

"Where's Elder Gunther?" Bridgot asked, looking at the group of elders.

"He is no longer our leader," he answered, "I'm afraid he passed away."

Bridgot looked to his family for confirmation, and they nodded.

"I am our Head Elder, now," he said, "I am Elder Carsen."

"Pleasure, I'm sure," Bridgot said, "I am *King* Bridgot, and this is my wife, *Queen* Celestia. I was born of this village. You may remember me. These," he gestured to the other three, "are our friends. We are on a quest of great importance, and we come seeking an item we need to fulfill it, which we've discovered is located here."

"Yes, I remember you," Elder Carsen said snidely, "You *married* to become king."

Bridgot drew his sword, pointing it at the old man, "Choose your words more wisely, peasant."

"Bridgot," his mother said, reprimanding him.

He lowered his sword, re-sheathing it and eyeing Elder Carsen meaningfully all the while.

"We shall hear your request tomorrow morning," he stated.

With that, the council dispersed, and Elder Lukehart whispered, "Good to see you again, sire." More loudly, he added, "We shall, of course, feast in your honor this evening."

"And, you shall, of course, stay with us," Bridgot's mother said, leading them back to the house.

"You've arrived just in time, brother," Luanne said, practically squealing with excitement, "The wedding is tomorrow."

"And, after tomorrow, I shall take over the farm," Bryan added, giving his younger brother a pat on the back.

"Yes," his mother said despondently, "Your father and I are ready to retire. We shall take the second guest house, and Bryan shall move his family into the main house. As you know, Margaret and her family will remain in the first guest house. Kyja lives with her husband, Ethan, their children, and his family. Luanne will move in with Dillon's family after the wedding, of course. So, you came at the right time."

Celestia squeezed her husband's arm, knowing what he was feeling.

"We have plenty of spare rooms at the moment," his mother added, "So, you all just take your pick."

They put the horses in the stable and went inside the house. The circular hut was just as it always was, and she felt their quest coming full circle, as they had been to all of the places they'd journeyed to on the first quest. It was decorated with a combination of dark colors and pastels, and had the main living area downstairs, with the bedrooms upstairs. She wondered if Bryan and Brianne would make any changes when they moved in. She guessed they might not recognize it on their next visit.

"Luanne is staying in Margaret's old room," his mother continued, "But, all the other rooms are vacant. You know your way upstairs. Why don't you show your friends to their rooms, and wash up for dinner." She turned to their three warriors, "Our village hosts magnificent feasts! You're in for a treat."

Bridgot led the way up the stairs of his parents' house, and to the bedrooms. When they reached the top, he showed them where the washroom was. "Celestia and I will stay in my old room. It's this one," he pointed to one of the rooms at the top of the ladder, on the small third floor of the hut, "There are two more rooms up here, and one room on this level."

"I'll take the one on this level," Thaandor said, "A man my age has no business climbing a ladder."

Xharia laughed, "I'm probably older than you."

"You never can tell with an elf," he replied, "But, I think I have you beat. I'm three hundred and twenty-two."

Xharia looked surprised, "One hundred and twelve."

Thaandor chuckled, "I'll go wash up."

"I'll take the middle room," Kgansten said.

"I suppose that leaves me with this one," Xharia said, climbing the ladder.

They all took turns washing up, and, by the time they were done, it was time for the feast. They went out to eat, taking their places together. Xharia found it difficult to eat, with the limited selection of fruits and vegetables. Celestia could tell she, like Aurano, had not eaten outside of the land of the elves before. *At least we aren't in the land of the dwarves*, she thought, *Then, she'd really have a difficult time.*

When the feast was over, and the celebration commenced, Bridgot pulled Celestia away. He led her back to the house and up to his room. "Remember when I brought you up here on our first quest?" he asked.

"Yes," she answered, looking out over the glowing village, "You wanted to show me the view of the village from your window."

"Remember how worried I was someone would catch us?" he laughed.

"We weren't married then," she said, "You didn't want anyone to get the wrong idea."

"Exactly," he said, moving closer.

She looked at him, then. He had a familiar look in his eyes, and they twinkled like a couple of lighthouses on a foggy sea. He cupped her face in his hand, kissing her. She leaned into him as he ran his fingers through her long, blonde hair.

"Should we be doing this?" she asked.

"No one will be home until after the celebration," he said, "We're alone; don't worry."

She chuckled, "What could they say if we weren't?"

He smiled, "Nothing. Not anymore."

With that, he kissed her again, leaning her back against the bed.

As everyone scurried about, making preparations for the wedding, Bridgot, Celestia, Thaandor, Kgansten, and Xharia headed to Town Hall to speak with the Council of Elders. It was the largest hut, situated at the center of the village. Inside, the council was waiting for them, seated around the table at the head of the room. The five of them strode over, taking the vacant chairs, leaving a few of the elders to stand.

"You say you have come seeking something from us?" Elder Carsen asked.

"Yes," Celestia answered, "It is of the utmost importance that you oblige."

"Oh?" he said, smirking.

"The fate of the entire world rests upon us fulfilling this quest," Bridgot snapped, "including this village."

"Wars, plagues, death, and destruction will be your reward if you refuse," Thaandor bellowed.

Elder Carsen paused, "What is it that you seek?"

"A weapon," Bridgot said, "It is located in our weapons depository. My wife is able to sense the weapons we need, and she feels its presence here."

"In order to destroy the powers of the dark wizard, Nazirdok," Celestia said, "according to The Oracle, we must have a weapon and warrior from each the five races of dwarf, elf, dragon rider, wizard, and human. We have all the warriors, and four of the five weapons. We need only the one here to fulfill our quest, and the prophecy."

"I see no wars," he said, "I see no plagues, nor death and destruction."

"Because you are blind to the world," Bridgot said, pounding his fist against the table, "Wars have broken out all across the land. The north of Gachichken fights Cardeas, war has spread across the kingdoms of Duwazo, a dark wizard commands the armies of Kogatsa, Mashang, and Kuttub, and that's only the wars we've seen since leaving home."

Elder Carsen drummed his fingers on the table, puckering his lips, and looking around at the assembled elders. "We shall grant no such request," he smirked.

"You don't have a choice," Bridgot said, "You're a mere Council of Elders. *We* are royalty."

"You rule a kingdom of Duwazo. Your authority does not stretch beyond that. The village of Kataran is under the command of *us*," he said, grinning.

"Then you claim responsibility for *everything* that happens as a result," Bridgot snarled.

"Perhaps you do not understand the gravity of the situation," Thaandor offered.

"Perhaps *you* do not understand the meaning of *no*," Elder Carsen fired back, "Now, get out of *my* Town Hall."

They all rose, and Bridgot flipped the table. The other elders looked scared, disheartened, and remorseful, like they wished they could help. Elder Carsen just sat smiling, knowing he'd won. He ignored the table, continuing about his business as if nothing had happened. Celestia was disgusted by his behavior.

They all left angrily, out into the square. The wedding preparations were almost complete. They could see the feast tables lined up, covered in white lace tablecloths, with floral centerpieces. There was an aisle in the center, with rows of chairs placed alongside it for the guests. An archway with white flowers was at the end of the white lace aisle runner.

Bridgot's family were all still bustling about, and Dillon's family were preparing on the opposite side of the square. Weddings were always a village event, and everyone was involved in the joining of two families.

"Bridgot!" his mother called, "Come on, we need a few extra hands!"

Though they were still seething, they headed over to assist them. Celestia knew Bridgot would never ruin his sister's wedding.

"Margaret's helping Luanne get ready. I need someone to help the little girls. Bethany, Theresa, and Jada are the flower girls. Celestia, would you and your lady friend help them please?" his mother asked.

"Certainly," Celestia said, sighing.

"Excellent," she said, "They're in the first guest house with the bride and bridesmaids."

Celestia and Xharia headed over to help the girls, as she heard his mother asking Bridgot and Kgansten to go check on the boys on the other side, and enlisting Thaandor to help her put the finishing touches on the decorations.

When they entered the expanded guest house, which belonged to Margaret and her family, it was full of girls rushing to get ready. Margaret was already in her bridesmaid dress—a pink frock with a bow tied around the waist—and had her hair done up with flowers in it. She was busy doing Luanne's hair. She sat in a chair in her wedding dress, which was simple and flowy with long, sheer sleeves and a high neck. Kyja, Anne Marie, and a couple of Luanne's friends were also dressed in bridesmaid dresses, helping each other with their hair. The little girls were chasing each other around, not even dressed yet.

"Bethany, Jada, Theresa," Celestia shouted, "front and center."

The three girls ran over, gawking at Xharia.

"Where are their dresses?" Celestia asked.

"On the couch," Margaret answered.

"Come on, girls," she said, leading them over to the living room. Xharia followed, and the two of them got the three girls dressed. By the time they were finished, the bridesmaids were ready, and Luanne's friends began doing the flower girls' hair.

"I'm glad you could all stay for the wedding," Kyja said, giving Celestia a hug.

"Me, too," Celestia said.

Kyja paused, "Then, why do you look so upset?"

She gestured toward the back door, and Celestia, Kyja, and Xharia slipped outside.

"The Council of Elders denied our request," Celestia said.

"I'm not surprised," Kyja said, "Life has been a lot more difficult for all of us since Elder Carsen took over."

"What is his problem?" she asked.

"I don't know," Kyja said, "I think he's just on a power trip since everyone preferred Elder Gunther."

"Well, he's standing in our way, and jeopardizing our whole quest," Celestia said.

Kyja looked from her to Xharia, and back to her, "What do you need, anyway?"

"We need a weapon from your weapons depository," she said.

"Without it, we're all doomed," Xharia added.

"Thank you, Xharia," Celestia said, looking at her meaningfully.

Kyja gave them another look, showing her confusion, "Why *our* weapons depository?"

"She can sense the weapons we need," Xharia said, "And, the one we need to complete this quest and fulfill the prophecy is here."

Kyja's eyes widened, "I thought the prophecy was already fulfilled."

"It's a long story," Celestia said, "But, in short, it hasn't been. We thought it had, too."

"Kyja!" Margaret yelled from the house, "Get your butt in here!"

"I'll help you," Kyja said, "Don't worry." With that, she rushed back into the house.

Xharia and Celestia looked at each other, hope and doubt on both their faces.

The five of them took their seats as the ceremony began. The flower girls went down the aisle, littering it with petals. Then, the bridal procession made their way to the end of the aisle. Three of the five groomsmen had red hair, and Celestia could tell they were related to the groom. She had never met Dillon's family before. The first time she'd even met Dillon himself was at Aurano's birthday party. The guys wore pink shirts with their brown peasant's pants and boots. All the decor was white, and all the flowers and outfits were pink.

When Luanne came out, they all rose, and she glided on air down the aisle, beaming a great smile. She held a bouquet that covered her plump belly, and there were white flowers tucked into her curled hair. Dillon smiled when he saw her, standing in his Sunday clothes at the end of the aisle, red hair glowing in the sunlight.

They said their vows, exchanged rings, and kissed, with the whole village erupting in cheers. Bridgot grasped Celestia's hand during the ceremony, and they shared a smile with each other, leaning against one another lovingly. In spite of the ever-present feeling of doom their quest caused within them, the light-hearted occasion allowed them a brief reprieve. Romance and merriment hung in the air of Kataran that night, and they were relieved to indulge in it for a while.

When the ceremony was over, everyone gathered at the tables for the feast. They all ate, enjoying loading themselves up with real food before the inevitable return journey. Poor Xharia wasn't able to enjoy as many things as the rest of them, but she also didn't have as far to go. When the food had been consumed, and the drinks started flowing, the dancing commenced. The five of them congratulated Luanne and Dillon personally, before joining the villagers on the dance floor.

Celestia was able to dance freely with Bridgot, without fear of judgment this time around. It brought back memories of when they'd danced in that village in Millhaymae after they'd liberated them from slavery. The music took control, and they twirled and dipped and moved in sync with each other. She felt the passion she'd felt then, and she could tell he felt it, too.

He locked eyes with her as he pulled her close, and she could feel his breath against her cheek. She gasped, looking into their gray depths. He started pulling her away from the dance floor, but they stopped when they heard something moving through the trees. Kyja emerged, waving for them to follow her away from the crowd. "Kyja," Celestia whispered.

"What is it?" he asked.

"Come on," she said, "Xharia and I explained the situation to her, and she said she'd help us. This might be it. Let's get the others."

The two of them subtly moved to Thaandor, Xharia, and Kgansten on the dance floor, each in turn, whispering for them to follow Kyja. One by one, they slipped away, and finally, Bridgot and Celestia followed, ducking into the shadows of the trees.

"Come on," Kyja whispered, leading them away from the celebration.

"Where are we going?" Bridgot asked.

"Do you want that weapon or not?"

"How do you intend to get it?" he questioned.

"I have my methods," she said, "I told you I dreamed of a more exciting life. This is my chance to help you on one of your quests, and I'm not missing it."

"What did you do?" he whispered.

"I stole the key to the weapons depository," she answered, "The whole village is at the wedding, getting drunk. It's the perfect opportunity to sneak in and take the weapon you need."

"Brilliant," Celestia said.

"I like your sister," Xharia added.

They reached the weapons depository, and Kyja pulled out the key, unlocking it. They snuck inside, and Celestia found the weapon. It was a sword, gleaming in the bit of moonlight that streamed in through the trees.

"This is the sword of Vidar the Conqueror," Bridgot said in awe.

"Really?" Celestia said, "Even I've heard of him."

"Who?" Kgansten asked.

"He's a famous human warrior," Bridgot answered, "He once took over 90% of the human realm, before a resistance force joined up with the elves, wizards, dragon riders, and dwarves to defeat him."

"Wow," Kgansten said, eyes widening, "I must say, I'm impressed."

"Let's do it now," Celestia said, "We have all the warriors, and all the weapons. We have the orb. Let's destroy it."

They went out into the forest, away from the weapons depository, not knowing exactly what would happen when the orb was destroyed. Thaandor unwrapped it, placing it on the ground.

Xharia's eyes widened, "So, that's where Nazirdok's powers are stored?"

Celestia handed each of them their weapon. Thaandor took the wand of Merlin, Kgansten took the axe of Kgoresh the Terrible, Xharia took Aurano's bow and arrow, Bridgot took the sword of Vidar the Conqueror, and Celestia took Ezmyra's talon. Kyja watched in wide-eyed amazement.

"Okay, I'll have to cast a spell over it," Thaandor said, "And then, you each need to strike it with your weapon in quick succession, and it will all be over."

They all nodded, readying themselves.

Thaandor pointed Merlin's wand at the orb, saying, "*Configlié!*" His silver stream of magic exploded from the wand, wrapping around the orb.

Xharia shot an arrow at it, and it glanced off.

Kgansten swung the axe down upon it.

Bridgot sliced at it with the sword.

Celestia plunged the talon into it.

They all stepped back, watching and waiting. And . . . nothing. Nothing happened. The orb remained, looking untouched. There wasn't a scratch on it.

"What happened?" Celestia exclaimed, "Why didn't it work?"

"I don't understand," Thaandor said, "We have all the weapons. We have all the warriors. It should have worked."

"What do we do now?" Kgansten asked.

"I must consult with The Oracle," Thaandor said.

"No!" Bridgot exclaimed, "She's the one that got us into this mess! We did what she said. It should have worked. But, it didn't!"

"Bridgot," Celestia said, "I know you're beside yourself. I am, too. But, we have to figure this out. Let's call The Oracle. Maybe it's a simple matter of a different order or incantation. We can fix this. Just call her, Thaandor."

Thaandor gathered a pool of water, calling The Oracle.

Her glowing face appeared on the surface, "Thaandor."

"You already know what I would ask," he said, "I hope you have the answer."

"I do," she said, "But you will not like it. I think, deep down, you already know what I would say."

Thaandor sighed, hanging his head.

"What is it?" Xharia asked.

Celestia came over to the puddle, "Tell me what we must do. And this time, don't leave anything out."

The Oracle smiled, "The orb can only be destroyed in the place it was created. You have, indeed, gathered the required warriors and weapons. You did nothing wrong. You're simply in the wrong place."

Celestia felt her heart sink into her feet, and she grew cold. She looked at her warriors, eyes wide.

"What?" Bridgot said in disbelief, "Are you saying we have to go back to Khanjgi to destroy it?"

"Yes," The Oracle answered, "Do this, and the prophecy will *finally* be completely fulfilled."

"Oh, yeah," Kgansten said mockingly, "Because it'll be such a nice, leisurely stroll back to Khanjgi! Do you have any idea the things we'll have to face?"

"We'll never get past my kingdom," Xharia said, "As soon as we set foot on elven soil, they'll catch us."

"The armies of the dark wizard have probably already infiltrated the dwarven tunnels," Kgansten said, "Even if they haven't, getting past them in Kuttub will be impossible."

"That's not even mentioning the fact that we'll have to face and defeat a dark wizard capable of wielding raw power, even if somehow we were able to reach Khanjgi!" Bridgot shouted.

The Oracle smiled, and her picture began to fade. "Trust your instincts, Celestia," was all she said before she vanished from the water's surface.

Thaandor looked up, "I'm sorry, all of you. We should have come here after the wizards and dragon riders, and worked our way up to Khanjgi. Perhaps if we hadn't gone there first, we'd stand a chance."

"It's not your fault, Thaandor," Celestia said.

They all sat in silence for a while, not sure what to do.

Finally, Xharia spoke up, "I didn't run away from home to give up. I came with you to see your quest through. This makes things harder, yes, but we can do it. We don't have a choice. Need I remind you what happens if we fail? Let's move out. Sneaking through the land of the elves undetected is our first challenge. Who's with me?"

Celestia looked up at the tall, graceful, elven woman. "I am," she said confidently.

"Me, too," Thaandor said.

"Aye," Kgansten agreed, "To victory, or death."

"Bridgot?" Celestia asked, looking at him.

"I believe in you," Kyja said, walking to Bridgot's side, "You can do anything. You're the most amazing person I know. I envy you. You got out of this village. You made something of yourself." She paused, looking at each of them, and then back to her brother, "I'd do anything to help you. But, I'm not cut out for war. I'm a mom, now. This is as far as I go. But you can go further." She stepped forward, hugging him, "Look at them." She waited for him to look at each of them, "They need you. Go."

Bridgot smiled at his sister, patting her arm.

She smiled back.

He turned toward the rest of them, "I'm in. Let's do this."

Of Unicorns and Elves

11

The five of them snuck off into the night with their horses, riding back toward Gliken. Kyja locked the weapons depository back up, returning the key and going back to the wedding, pretending that nothing happened.

They found a spot far enough from the village to make camp, and Thaandor cast protective enchantments around their campsite. Celestia thought to herself, *We're going to need a lot more energy if we are to succeed.* When she stored her energy for the night, she also drew energy from everyone else, except Kgansten, who was taking the first watch. She decided she would do that each night, to increase her stores more.

The only one who noticed was Thaandor, since he felt the pull on his own magic. He looked at her suspiciously, but didn't say anything. Celestia guessed he knew what she was trying to do, and agreed with her. This quest was bound to require all the energy she could amass before it was over.

As she slept, Celestia dreamt that she was at the castle in Khanjgi. Everything was sort of hazy, but she went to the room with all her warriors. They set down the orb and pulled out the weapons. And, one by one, they disappeared. She panicked, looking around, and calling their names. Then, through the mist, Zandor appeared. She stared in horrified surprise as he grinned, and his fangs grew out of his mouth. He started laughing, and his eyes turned pitch black, spreading across his face. Soon, he was a faceless void of raw power, spreading its darkness through the empty space. Its tentacles reached the orb, and the glass vanished, releasing the powers within.

The figure grew, and, out of it, stepped Nazirdok. He grinned, casting a spell at Celestia, and everything went black.

She woke in a cold sweat, jumping up. Everyone was asleep except for Bridgot, since it was his watch. She struggled to catch her breath, hyperventilating.

"Celestia?" Bridgot said worriedly, rushing to her side, "What is it? What's wrong?"

She couldn't formulate words, and instead, latched onto him, holding him tight.

He wrapped his arms around her, "It's alright. Everything's alright. You're safe. Shh, it was just a dream."

"I saw him," she said.

"Who?"

"I saw Nazirdok. It was Zandor, but he morphed into Nazirdok when he took the powers from the orb. He made all of you disappear."

Bridgot pulled her into him again, rubbing her back soothingly.

"He made all of you disappear," she said again.

"It was just a dream," he said, "We're all right here." He kissed her head, gently pressing her to his chest.

"It was so real," she said.

"It's alright," he replied.

They stood like that for a while, before Celestia said, "Bridgot?"

"Yes?"

"What if that was an omen? What if this quest is doomed to fail? What if we're playing right into his hands, bringing the orb back to Khanjgi?"

He sighed, "It's a risk we'll have to take. What's our alternative?"

"I wish we had one," she said.

"Me, too," he agreed, holding her tight, "Me, too."

They rode all day the following day, nearing Gliken by nightfall. As they approached the area, and Celestia felt the pull of magic in the forest, Xharia whispered, "We should move through now, while it's night, to avoid detection. It's our best chance of getting through Garellis."

"She's right," Thaandor whispered, "Let's go."

The five of them entered Gliken, quietly moving through the kingdom of Garellis. The mermaids splashing in the darkened river and the soft hum of the pixies were the only sounds. The light the pixies gave off, along with the moonlight, were all they had to illuminate their path. Celestia saw the unicorn again, watching them from the trees.

"That's amazing," Xharia whispered, "Unicorns rarely watch over people."

"This is going to sound crazy," Celestia said, "But, I can feel the pull of its magic."

"You're just full of surprises, aren't you?" Thaandor asked, "It is a rare gift, indeed, to sense unicorns."

Celestia stared at the creature, watching the way it slid its hoof across the ground and nodded its head at her, "I think it's trying to tell me something."

Suddenly, the guards of the elven forest appeared, and, before they could say anything, lifted reeds to their lips, blowing out tranquilizing darts into their necks. Celestia slumped against Razel as she lost consciousness.

When she woke, she was in irons, kneeling before King Boreas. Her warriors were all with her, shackled the same. The elven warriors had formed a circle around them, swords pointed their direction.

"So," King Boreas said, "This is how you repay me for my generosity? Sneaking around my kingdom in the night, kidnapping my daughter?"

"They didn't kidnap me," Xharia said, "I ran after them. I wanted to help them."

"Silence, Xharia!" he snapped, "You're in enough trouble as it is." He paused, "I offered you food and shelter. I gave you special permission to borrow an elven weapon from our museum. On your last quest, I granted you an elven warrior, who was killed helping you. And yet, you took my daughter, too."

Celestia exchanged glances with her warriors, unsure what the elf king would do. Finally, she looked over at Xharia. She looked back at her remorsefully, apologizing with her eyes.

"The four of you will be locked in the dungeons until an appropriate punishment can be decided," he said, "Take them away. As for you, Xharia, you will be on lock-down in your room for the next five years. You will be forbidden to go anywhere, or do anything, until I believe you've learned your lesson."

The guards lifted all of them from the ground, leading them from the throne room. Xharia shouted the whole way, as she was dragged deeper into the palace, to her room. The four of them were taken up to the treetops, where the cells of the dungeon were formed—so high up, they wouldn't be able to get down safely, even if they found a way to break out.

They were each tossed into a separate cell, and the doors were magically sung into place, forming a solid cage wall, rather than simply being locked. Celestia looked around at the gnarled tree walls and floor, which were impenetrable, and the two walls comprised of bars. On one side, it overlooked the stairwell, and the other cells of the elven dungeon. On the other, she could see down to the ground of the elven city—the whole, long way down it was.

When the guards had departed, and they were alone, Thaandor's voice came into her cell, "Celestia?"

"Yes?" she asked, "I'm here, Thaandor. What is it?"

"I'd like to teach you a new spell."

"No offense, Thaandor, but this isn't really the best time," she said.

"On the contrary," he said, "Now is the perfect time."

She sighed, "What spell is it?"

"Teleportation," he answered.

"Tele-what?"

"Teleportation," he said again, "The art of going from one place to another instantaneously."

Celestia gasped, "I thought you said no wizard could do that."

"No," he replied, "I said no wizard could transport four people and their horses from Abyumo to Kogatsa. But, transporting one person at a time from inside a cell to outside a cell is possible."

"What are we waiting for?" she asked, "Let's do it."

"It's a very advanced spell," he said, "Perhaps the most advanced spell. I've never seen anyone get it on the first try. We could still be stuck here a while. I'd use my magic, but, in my old age my energy has waned. I can't perform the spells I once could. I may be able to get myself out, but I couldn't get everyone out."

She nodded, even though he couldn't see her, "I'm ready."

"Guys, before you bust us out," came Bridgot's voice, "maybe we should come up with a plan. Once we're out of the cages, what are we going to do? How are we going to get past the dungeon guards? How are we going to find Xharia, the horses, and our supplies, including the weapons? We've got to be able to do all of that before we just bust out of here. Otherwise, we'll be sitting ducks, standing around the dungeon until the guards come back and get better cells."

"Hmm," Thaandor said, "Good point."

"How far can I teleport everyone?" Celestia asked, "And, where can I? Do I have to know where we're going? Or, can I focus on what we hope to find there?"

"Your energy determines how far you can teleport," Thaandor answered, "The amount of strength required is the same amount it would take you to carry however many people you're transporting across whatever distance you're attempting to traverse."

Celestia thought a moment, "I think I have a plan, then. What's the spell?"

"Take it easy," he said, "You don't want to over-exert yourself. You don't know what you're capable of, yet."

"There's only one way to find out," she replied.

Thaandor sighed, "Very well. To teleport, you must visualize very clearly in your mind where you are, feeling the presence of the room around you, and your magic flowing through you. Then, you must visualize who, what, or where you're trying to go, very clearly. When you have it, say, "*Momento.*"

Celestia focused, tapping into her raw powers, and visualizing the cell around her, feeling its presence. Then, she focused on the stairwell outside, visualizing it clearly, "*Momento.*" She felt herself moving, as if through a windstorm, and she opened her eyes. She was sitting on the opposite end of her cell.

"How'd your first attempt go?" Thaandor asked.

"I moved from one side of the cell to the other," she answered.

He laughed, "I told you no one gets it on their first try. But, honestly, that was good for your first attempt. Try again."

Twenty-five attempts later, she had been all the way around her cell three times. "It's hopeless," she said, "Are you sure I'm not missing something?"

"I haven't trained you on anything this advanced before," he responded, "It takes a lot of practice. It doesn't have to do with your energy or power level. It has to do with your focus and your detailed visualization. Directing your powers is harder with this spell than any other. Your wand would be very helpful right about now."

"Yes, well, they took it, along with everything else," she said.

"I know," he said, "So, you'll just have to keep working on it. Focus on each little detail when you're visualizing. You should know every detail of your cell by now, as many times as you've circled it." He chuckled.

She sighed, trying to focus her mind again. Just then, the door to the dungeon opened, and there were footsteps on the stairs. *Oh no,* she thought, *Sounds like King Boreas has figured out what to do with us.* She looked out of her cell, trying to see who it was.

One of the guards was coming up the stairs, and he pushed a plate of food through the cage bars, moving through the dungeon. It was bread and water—the meal of prisoners. Celestia looked at it, discouraged. She pushed it away, curling up in a ball to sleep and recover her strength.

A couple of days went by as she kept trying to master the spell for teleportation. Thaandor even tried to teleport her out of her cell, so she could find another way to free the rest of them, but he couldn't muster the strength.

I wonder when he will decide our punishment, Celestia thought, staring at the wall of her cell. Suddenly, she heard footsteps on the stairs. *Mealtime,* she thought, sighing in frustration.

When she looked out of her cell, one of the guards stood before her, "King Boreas requests an audience with you." He unsung her cell door, yanking her out.

"It's about time," Kgansten said.

"Just you," the guard said.

Celestia looked back at her warriors as he dragged her out of the dungeon. He led her back to King Boreas' throne room, pushing her before him.

He stood tall and proud, looking wrathful.

She looked up at him, uncertain.

"I have decided on your punishment," he said.

Celestia braced herself.

"You will remain in our dungeons until the last star of your quest falls," he said, "Then, you'll be free to go, along with the knowledge that you failed for your betrayal."

"No," she said, moving toward him.

The guards grabbed her quickly, dragging her from the throne room.

"You're making a terrible mistake!" she shouted, "It doesn't have to be this way!"

They dragged her all the way back to the cell, casting her inside, and resealing the door.

"No!" she yelled as they descended the stairs, locking the dungeon behind them.

"What is it?" Bridgot asked.

"He made his decision, I take it," Thaandor stated.

"Yes," Celestia said, "We are to remain locked up until the last star falls, and our quest is failed. Only then shall he release us."

Kgansten yelled, shaking the bars of his cell.

Celestia felt the hopelessness of her warriors penetrating her cage. Moonlight was coming through the trees, and she realized there was nothing further she could do that night. She sighed, lying down in the cell. There was nothing more she could accomplish without energy. She curled up against the wall, drifting off to sleep.

Celestia awoke to the sound of footsteps on the stairs. When she looked through her cage bars, she realized it was still night. She craned her neck to see who was coming at this hour. Before her eyes, the unicorn appeared, with Xharia on its back.

"How did you do that?" Celestia asked in amazement.

Xharia laughed, "I was working on a plan to get you guys out. I climbed out of my bedroom window, and I was working out how to steal the keys from the guards when he came up to me, nudging me with his snout. I knew he wanted to help us, and I remembered what you said about him trying to talk to you. So, I climbed upon his back, and he brought me here. His magic somehow shielded us from the guards, because they didn't see us."

"How?" Celestia asked, "How can unicorns use magic?"

"The same as dragons, I suppose," Xharia answered, "Their whole beings are made up of magic. But, enough chit-chat. Let's get you guys out."

The unicorn touched its horn to the cage wall of Celestia's cell, and it disappeared.

She gawked in amazement, locking eyes with the unicorn, "Wow. Thank you."

He nodded, whinnying, and then freed Thaandor, Bridgot, and Kgansten.

"Let's go," Xharia said, "Everyone, place your hand upon him. So long as you're in contact with the unicorn, you won't be seen."

They all stared in amazement, placing their hands upon the unicorn, and walking out of the dungeon. They went right past the guards, and not one of them was seen. They walked along, following where the unicorn led. He took them right to their supplies, which were in King Boreas' bedroom. It was even larger than his throne room, with one of the largest beds Celestia had ever seen. No one was in it at the moment, much to their relief. They gathered their food, clothes, and weapons hurriedly. Then, it led them to the stable, where their horses were waiting.

"What is your name?" Celestia asked.

The others looked at her as though she were crazy.

Ceres, the thought floated through Celestia's mind. "Ceres?" she asked.

The unicorn whinnied and nodded.

"Are you the one who's been keeping an eye on us from the forest?"

He nodded again.

"Thank you," she said, "And, thank you for helping us."

Her warriors stared at her in amazement, exchanging glances with one another. But, there was no time to waste. They loaded their supplies quickly, leaping upon their horses' backs. As Xharia dismounted, Ceres galloped away, into the forest. The five of them rode hard, out of the stable, off into the night. Leaving Garellis behind them, they only looked back when they heard another explosion, as a star fell right through the dungeon.

Xharia

12

The next day, they made their way through Gliken, riding hard. They knew they didn't have much time, and every second was costly in their race against the stars. There were only two left, looming over them like scornful enemies. It was only a two days' ride out of Gliken. They got through quickly, passing the incredible creatures of the elven forest once more. When they reached the dwarven tunnels in Korga, the guards allowed them inside. They rode into Dirthix, to take shelter with King Thanghor one last time.

"Lord Kgansten," Seamus whispered, coming up to them, "You must leave here at once. Go with haste!"

"Why?" Kgansten asked, "What's going on?"

"King Thanghor has quite lost his mind," Seamus answered, "He's labeled you a traitor, and says you stole the axe of Kgoresh the Terrible. Furthermore, he refuses to send our troops to aid our fellow dwarven kingdoms."

"Then, the armies *have* gotten in?"

Seamus nodded, "They are pouring in steadily through the other entrances, and occupying the kingdoms therein."

Kgansten paused, scratching his red-bearded chin. "Thank you, Seamus," he said finally.

"What do we do?" Xharia asked.

"I'm sorry, Kgansten," Celestia said, "I feel like it's my fault. We should have said something to him before we left, like you wanted to."

"It's not your fault, lass," Kgansten said. After a pause, he added, "We should do as Seamus says. There's no telling how long we'll be able to remain undetected."

They all nodded, riding through Dirthix with haste. They got past the palace, starting to ride hard into the main hallway. The guards of the hall spotted them, whispering to each other. After a tense pause, they nodded to them, indicating they would allow them to pass. The five of them nodded back, relieved. They rode as fast as they could, trying to make their way out of Dirthix. It would take a few days, but they had no choice.

When they stopped to make camp, they stuck to the shadows, keeping out of sight. Thaandor shielded them with magic, and Celestia stored their energy again. They knew it would take them over a fortnight to make it through the tunnels, and that wasn't even considering Zandor's army.

They rode the next few days, reaching Kgansten's house again. He welcomed them inside, and they relished the escape, and the relative safety.

"You have a beautiful home," Xharia said.

"Thank you," Kgansten said, nodding to her. He led them upstairs, and they all washed up, occupying his guest rooms.

When they were alone, Celestia risked another call to her mother.

"Celestia," her mother whispered, "How's everything going?"

"We have everything we need," Celestia answered, "But, apparently, we have to go back to Khanjgi to complete our quest. It's a long story. We're at Kgansten's house now. We went through the land of the elves twice, and Bridgot's village, since the last time we talked. We were even able to attend Luanne's wedding whilst we were there. Though, we didn't go there to frolic. One of the things we needed was there."

"You've traveled very far," her mother replied, "Back to Khanjgi, you say?"

Celestia could hear the worry in her mother's voice. "We'll be alright," she said, "We have to end this. It's the only way." After a brief pause, she added, "Are you guys still safe? Is everyone alright?"

Lady Eva nodded, "The children are perfectly fine. They're asleep right now. Natasha just got her boys to settle down. We're still in the safe-house. I just hope they haven't trashed the castle too terribly."

"Me, too," she agreed, "But, it's more important that you guys are safe."

"Finish your quest and come home," Eva said, "Your children miss you." She looked at Bridgot, "Both of you."

Bridgot looked away.

"We'll do what we can," Celestia said, "We love you all. Tell our kids we love them. And tell Kgansten's family he loves them."

"I will," she said, "But don't talk that way. It makes me think you aren't coming back."

"Sorry," she replied, "But, just make sure they know. Just in case."

Her mother looked at her, "Be careful, Celestia. You, too, Bridgot."

"We will," Bridgot said.

"We've got to go," Celestia added.

"Okay," Eva replied, eyes welling up, "I love you guys. Good luck."

With that, Celestia severed the connection, and she and Bridgot sighed heavily, feeling the same. They knew what dangers lie ahead. They were well aware of the possibility they wouldn't return. Yet, they had no choice. They couldn't turn around and go home. If they didn't complete this quest, they'd have no home to go to.

They lied down to sleep, tossing and turning the whole night. They found it hard to sleep with all the thoughts their minds were plagued with. In the end, their tired bodies won, and they faded out of consciousness.

The next day, they continued their two-week journey out of Korga. They weren't sure what challenges the dwarven tunnels would hold for them this time around, but they knew they'd have to face them together. Xharia looked particularly nervous, as she had since entering the tunnels. Celestia recalled how Aurano had been when they'd journeyed through with him, and she knew it was simply a matter of being an elf in dwarven territory.

Due to the increasing risk of attack in the night, Celestia went back to only storing her own energy, and leaving everyone else's, so they'd be strong enough to fight if need be. They journeyed a few days deeper into the caves, making steady progress. They stuck to the shadows as much as possible, peering around corners, and trying to avoid detection.

Celestia continued working with Thaandor, learning spells for magical combat, and preparing herself for the inevitable battle with Zandor. When she took her shift at night, she secretly practiced the spell for teleportation, trying to master it.

One night, as she was teleporting herself across the hall, she heard voices coming up the corridor. They were being followed. She hurried to wake the others, and they armed themselves, trying to fully wake up.

"They went this way," one of them whispered.

"I don't like this," another voice said.

"Shut up," the first one replied, "King Thanghor gave us orders. Let's go."

Kgansten gasped.

As they watched, the group of guards from Dirthix rounded the corner, axes raised. When they saw the five of them awake and armed, they shrieked with surprise, backing up quickly. Kgansten let out a battle cry, charging forward. Bridgot joined him, followed by Xharia. Celestia lingered back, knowing her energy stores were low, since she'd already drained most of them, and was practicing magic on her shift with what little remained. Thaandor stayed by her side for protection, casting spells to aid the others.

"How could you?" Kgansten shouted, "You're my kin!"

"We are guards of the king!" the dwarf shouted back, "We follow our king's orders, to whatever end!"

Kgansten yelled, axe clashing with axe, knocking the dwarf back. "To whatever end?" he asked, "Even if that means killing his own nephew? Do you not see that he has gone mad? To follow his orders now is to give in to madness!"

The dwarf grabbed his axe, swinging it up toward Kgansten. He blocked it, knocking it from his hands, "I can't kill my own. Unlike you, I do not believe we are enemies. Go with peace, brother. Return home to *our* king."

Kgansten turned to walk away, but the dwarf got up, grabbing his axe to bring it down upon his back. Suddenly, an arrow hit him in the chest, and he stumbled back, collapsing. They turned to see who fired it, and saw that it was Xharia.

"You're more like Aurano than I thought," Kgansten said.

Xharia smiled, nodding to him.

They continued to fight, cutting down the soldiers until the rest finally fled.

As they sat down, trying to rest again before the dawn, Kgansten wore an expression that looked empty and broken, letting a single tear flow from his brown eyes down his ruddy cheek.

"I'm sorry, Kgansten," Celestia said, sitting beside him, "I know how hard that was for you."

"I lost many kin this night," he said, monotone, "And, I didn't have to." His voice grew emotional as he spoke, "They didn't have to die. My uncle's madness is destroying my homeland. He refuses to send our troops to defend our people from the invading army. He's labeled me—his own nephew—a traitor, and sent his guards to kill me. They were good dwarves, just following orders . . . orders from an unfit king."

"You know," she said softly, "sometimes people do things they wouldn't normally do when they're afraid. Your uncle is a good man. He loves you. He loves your people. He's just . . . making terrible decisions, because he's afraid."

"We're all afraid," Kgansten said, "But, we still do what we have to do. As a king, he can't afford to let fear rule him the way a commoner might."

"You're right," she replied, "Royals don't have the same luxuries as commoners in times like this. We must stay strong and do what's best for our people. Sometimes, we don't always know what that is. I just hope when this quest is over, the two of you can reconcile. He's in the wrong, yes, but you are family."

"I know," he said, "But, when this is over, I may have to overthrow him, for the good of our people."

She nodded, "We all have to do what we think is right, however tough a decision that might be."

He looked down.

She patted his back, heading back to her post.

"I'll start my watch, now," Bridgot said, intercepting her, "Get some rest. You need it more than I do."

She gave him a nod, settling down to sleep, thinking of what would become of Kgansten and Thanghor's relationship when this quest was over.

As they rode along the next day, Xharia guided her steed beside Kgansten, "You fought very bravely yesterday . . . for a dwarf."

Kgansten shot her a wry smile, "As did you . . . for an elf."

She smiled, "With the skills everyone here possesses, what army could offer us a challenge?"

He scoffed, "None. We are the finest warriors of each race there is."

"Exactly. We shouldn't fear Zandor. He should fear us!"

"Aye!" Kgansten agreed, raising his axe in the air. After a pause, he said, "You know, you remind me of Aurano."

"I see why he liked you," Xharia replied, "I hope we can be friends as well."

"Aye," he said again, "I think we can."

She smiled, "Good."

Celestia was relieved to see Kgansten smile again. She was glad he and Xharia were able to become friends, as he had with Aurano. In spite of the trials they faced, she knew the five of them would remain friends 'til the end of their days, however long that may be.

"Xharia, why don't you tell us a bit about yourself," Celestia said, "We hardly know anything about you."

"There's not much to tell," Xharia replied, "I grew up in Garellis, amongst the other elven children. My mother, Annalisa, my two sisters, and I were hidden from outsiders all my life by my father. He never introduced us to anyone outside of Garellis. My older sister, Gizella, adapted beautifully. She's to be queen one day, when our father steps down. She's always been the family favorite. She's beautiful, admired by all. She has many friends and suitors. She enjoys the luxuries of the palace, and spends a lot of time with our mother. She likes gossiping, dressing in nice, new clothes, and organizing parties."

"Sounds like a lot of the women in Duwazo," Celestia said.

"I can't speak from experience," Xharia said, "But, I'm sure her behavior is common. My younger sister, Kamine, is very studious. She's dedicated her life to the pursuit of knowledge. She's devoured countless books, and spends her days either in the library or at the Tree of Knowledge. We hardly ever see her. As for me, I've spent my time training. I've wanted to be an elven warrior my whole life. I've always admired our warriors for their speed and grace in combat. Suffice it to say my first elven tournament changed my life. I trained with my friends often, but no one was as dedicated to training as I was. Well, no one but Aurano. He was even more dedicated. I still spent my free time at parties, exploring the forest, and caring for its creatures. Yet, he was always training."

"The only thing he did for fun was watch the sunrise each day," Celestia said.

Xharia looked at her, "How'd you know that?"

"He told me," she replied, "We all traveled together quite a while. He told us all about himself, and we told him about us."

"Yes," she said, "I suppose I hadn't thought that you all had talked so much."

"We can't journey *every* day in silence," Celestia laughed, "But, honestly, I hoped it would bring us closer."

"Did it?" she asked.

"Yes," Kgansten answered, "It certainly did."

Celestia looked down.

"I was a peasant," Bridgot said suddenly, "stuck in my older brother's shadow. I was scholarly, and I solved the unsolvable riddle, becoming the warrior of the prophecy, destined to help the princess save the world from darkness. I have a big family. You met them all back in my village. Anyway, I fell in love with Celestia, and I married her and became a king. I became a husband." He looked at her, "I became a father."

Celestia smiled, "Yes, you did." She turned to Xharia, "I was a runaway princess, sick of royal life. We have much in common. I found out I was the princess of the prophecy, and it changed my life. I fell in love with Bridgot, and made friends of every race along the way. I somehow stopped Nazirdok's ritual, and found out I'm a witch. Now, I'm a queen, wife, and mother. And, I have to save the world again, from the same evil as before. And, again, I have all of you to help me."

Xharia smiled.

"I was a dwarven warrior," Kgansten said, "who dreamed of doing what my father couldn't, and becoming a Dwarf Lord. I did it, thanks to our last quest. But, I didn't feel the way I thought I would when I got everything I ever wanted. I think it was because, after losing our dear friends, it didn't hold the same importance to me. But, then I met my wife, Natasha, and we had our sons, and now, life has meaning again. I'm motivated to finish this quest for them. That's the thing I have to hold on to."

They all nodded, riding silently for a moment, before Thaandor said, "I was a young wizard, with no sense of purpose or direction, until I met The Oracle. I decided that's what I wanted to do with my long life, and I became her keeper. In my free time, I facilitate relations between the races, most particularly the wizards and dragon riders. I enjoy growing things like the elves, and reading. I've been around a long time, and read a lot of books."

Celestia chuckled, "I'm sure you have." She realized they'd never really asked Thaandor about himself. As they rode, she felt the strength of the group around her, and knew it would take a great foe to face them and win. Unfortunately, she knew that Zandor was, indeed, a great foe.

The days dragged by slowly, as they continued through the dwarven tunnels, trying to make it to Khanjgi before the last star fell. Celestia was feeling pretty good about her training, and, one night, Thaandor said, "I've taught you all I can. Now, it's up to you to use what you've learned, think on your feet, and counter the attacks that are launched at you."

Just like sword fighting and archery, Celestia thought.

"Why don't I help you practice?" Thaandor said.

Celestia shot him a questioning look, "You mean . . . fight you?"

"Yes," he said, "It will be the best training you can do right now. Obviously, we won't use any spells designed to kill. But, we can still practice blocking, and energy blasts, and reading your opponent."

She looked around at her other warriors. They all looked like they'd rather be anywhere else.

"Very well," she said, "Let's practice."

Thaandor smiled, "You three take the horses, and go around the corner. That way, we don't accidentally injure anyone."

Bridgot, Kgansten, and Xharia led the horses around the corner, peering back around to watch.

Thaandor went across the hall, leaving Celestia standing a ways from him, "When you're ready."

She drew her wand, preparing herself.

Thaandor cast a curse at her, and she threw up her magical barrier, blocking it. She engaged in the fight, blocking and blasting, keeping up with him well. She knew she had raw powers on the back burner, and he wouldn't stand a chance against them. But, she also knew not using them in this duel would better prepare her to face Zandor. Using raw powers against him would be the same as not using them against Thaandor.

They fired spells back and forth, lighting up the dwarven corridor with blue and silver magic. It was just like any other form of combat, which made it easier for Celestia to master dueling. Reading her opponent was the same across all types of fighting, from sword fighting to archery to axes to fists. She knew how to read her opponents when she fought with a sword, and how to gauge distances when she fired her arrows. Magic was like a combination of the two. The challenge excited her, and she relished the opportunity to test herself. In the end, she broke through Thaandor's barrier and knocked him back.

"Touché," he said, "Well done."

Celestia nodded, smiling, "I had a good teacher."

He came over, sitting down to catch his breath.

"You guys can come back, now," Celestia said, sitting beside Thaandor, "Are you alright?"

He nodded, "Just need to catch my breath. I'm an old man, remember?"

She laughed.

The other three came back around the corner, gathering around their campsite.

"That was terrifyingly impressive," Kgansten said.

"I never knew humans could wield such power," Xharia added, "even ones with magical abilities."

"You did well," Bridgot said, "Zandor should be afraid."

"Indeed you did," Thaandor agreed, "I only wish you had a more powerful practice partner."

"You're the most powerful wizard I know," Celestia said.

"I'm the *only* wizard you know."

"And, the only one I trust to teach me," she said.

He smiled. After a pause, he said, "Alright, everyone get some rest. We have only a few more days before we reach the exit to the tunnels, and undoubtedly, the awaiting army."

They journeyed quietly the next few days, not wanting to attract too much attention. They weren't sure how far the armies had gotten, or when they'd run into them. Celestia stopped storing energy at night altogether, conserving her strength for the fight ahead. She hoped she had enough energy stored up to defeat Zandor. She wished she did have a practice partner who could compare to his power level, to truly test her, as Thaandor had said. But, if they were the only two who could wield raw power, they were each on their own for training. At least she knew that he no longer had a mentor to teach him, since Nazirdok was gone.

The days grew darker, even in the tunnels, and they felt the heavy presence of hopelessness hanging in the air around them. As they rode, they were weighed down by it, and it drained their smiles and laughter away.

When they reached the final kingdom before the exit, a dwarven woman ran up to them. She had curly, red hair and a crazed look in her eyes.

"Turn back," she pleaded, "Turn back before it's too late."

"We're on a quest," Kgansten said, "We have no choice but to pass this way."

"There's no way out," she said, "Soldiers. Soldiers everywhere. They're at every entrance. They've destroyed this kingdom. They've destroyed my village."

"Go south, to the kingdom of Dirthix," Kgansten said, "Take any survivors with you. You'll be safe there. They have not yet reached it."

"You are fools," the woman said, "Leave while you still can."

They looked at each other.

"Let us ride through with haste before we draw too much attention," Thaandor said.

They all nodded, starting to ride away from the woman as swiftly as they could. Just then, the soldiers appeared in front of them, weapons drawn. The five of them leapt from their horses' backs, arming themselves. The woman ran down the corridor manically, screaming the whole way. The soldiers didn't bother to chase her. They cared not for the dwarven people. Their main targets were Celestia and her warriors—the only ones who could destroy Nazirdok's powers.

The soldiers charged in, starting their attack. Celestia and her warriors fought them off, beginning the battle. Bridgot thrusted, parried, and jabbed with his sword, cutting them down, and watching his wife's back. Kgansten swung his axe, eager to kill their enemies and prove that dwarves were to be taken seriously in combat. Xharia and Celestia fired off arrows, thinning out the horde of soldiers. Thaandor blasted them back with his magic, taking many of them out.

There were thousands of them, as they were comprised of three countries. The fight wore on, slowly working on their stamina. Celestia could see they couldn't win, and she began to look for an escape route.

"Bridgot," she said, swinging her sword, "We need a way out. Any bright ideas?"

He looked around, "Not at the moment." He ran his sword through several soldiers, looking around again, "There's no clean exit."

"If we retreat, they'll only chase us," Thaandor said, "We're their primary targets. They're not going to let us get away."

"What do we do?" Celestia asked.

"Kill the bastards!" Kgansten yelled, chopping through several of them with his axe.

They fought hard, but they were overwhelmed by the sheer number of opponents, and they were disarmed, as the soldiers captured them. They shackled the five of them together, leading them and their horses to the dwarven village they'd taken over. They were thrown into a large cage, and their horses were situated in a nearby corral.

"Great!" Bridgot said, "What do we do now?"

"We wait until they open the doors, and we kill them all!" Kgansten shouted.

"As thought-provoking a plan as that is," Thaandor said, "We cannot. We tried that approach already, and this is where it's gotten us. It's only a matter of time before they come for the orb."

Celestia looked forlornly through the cage bars, wishing she could figure out how to master the teleportation spell.

"There are no unicorns to save us this time," Xharia said.

Kgansten let out a yell of frustration.

Thaandor sighed.

They all sat down in the cage, unable to escape, each lost in their own thoughts.

It would take a miracle to get us out of here, Celestia thought, *Let's hope it happens fast, because we're running out of time.*

A Losing Battle

13

As her warriors slept, Celestia lay awake, staring through the bars of the cage. The soldiers had posted guards outside their cage during the night, to ensure they didn't escape. One of them was seated close to where Celestia lay.

"Can I ask you something?" she said.

He turned to look at her, a confused expression on his face.

"Why do you serve Zandor? What do you get out of the deal? How does a single man command the armies of three countries?"

"I am a soldier," he answered, staring proudly ahead, "We all are. When we are called to battle, we respond. Our commanders are whom we serve. If Zandor enlists their services, he enlists us all."

"What would make your commanders respond to his call?" she asked.

"I don't know," he snapped, "I'm not them. I would guess that they fear him, for his power is both awesome and terrible."

Celestia paused, "Do you not have a mind of your own? Do you not believe in right and wrong?"

He turned to look at her again, "True soldiers can't afford to think that way. No war is ever right. You're on one side or the other because of the commander you serve. Who's right and wrong doesn't matter. All that matters is you're alive to fight another day."

She looked away, "Right and wrong matters to me. The war itself may not be right, but the side you choose is. You shouldn't base that solely on your commander."

"Who said I care about being on the 'right' side?" he asked, "I care about being on the winning side, so I can go home to my family. Zandor will win. He's powerful, and he commands armies too large for anyone to defeat."

"You're part of those armies," she said.

"Exactly," he replied, "Which means I'm on the winning side."

"What about my family?" she said softly, "How will I go home to them?"

"Sorry you chose the losing side," he retorted, "You should have chosen differently."

"I care about the world being plunged into darkness," she said angrily, grabbing the cage, "There won't be a home to go back to when this is over; nowhere to rest safely, away from the darkness. I ask you, what kind of a world do you want to raise your children in? You're doing this for your family. I am, too."

He didn't reply, but stood to walk away. Before he did, he turned back around, "I won't allow your silver tongue to make me a traitor." He switched posts with another soldier, going to his tent.

She knew she had made an impact, but she also knew he would not waiver. They would receive no aid from these men. They were truly enemies, ready to fight for a cause they didn't care whether they agreed with. She sighed, looking at her sleeping warriors. *I can't lose them*, she thought, *One way or another, we have to win.*

She looked at her husband, appreciating his sleeping face. She gritted her teeth, determined, *One way or another . . .*

That night, Celestia had another dream. She was at the castle in Khanjgi again. Everything was hazy, and she went to the room with all her warriors. They set down the orb and pulled out the weapons. Through the mist, Zandor appeared. She stared in horrified surprise as he grinned, and his fangs grew out of his mouth. He started laughing, and his eyes turned pitch black, spreading across his face. Soon, he was a faceless void of raw power, spreading its darkness through the empty space. Its tentacles reached the orb, and the glass vanished, releasing the powers within. He was consumed by dark magic, and, out of it, stepped Nazirdok. This time, the dream was different. As she looked at Nazirdok's face, it changed again. When it took shape, it was her own face. She screamed as the other her began to kill off her warriors, one by one. The other her looked at her with an evil grin, laughing. She tried to fight her off, blasting her with wave after wave of raw power. But, the other her was too strong. She was left alone, trying to fight, as the figure changed from her to Nazirdok to Zandor and back again. It even took the forms of each of her warriors, all laughing maniacally. She sent a blast of light through it, and it exploded, covering her in darkness.

"Celestia," Bridgot was saying, "Celestia. It's okay. You're okay. Wake up."

She opened her eyes, jolting up. She was covered in a cold sweat again, and she looked at the faces of her warriors. They were all awake, staring at her in worry.

"What? What is it?" she asked.

"I would ask you the same thing," Bridgot said.

"What do you mean?"

"You were screaming in your sleep," he said.

She took a few deep breaths, trying to calm herself, "I'm sorry, you guys. I didn't mean to wake you."

"It's alright, Celestia," Xharia said, "We're mostly just worried about you."

"I'm okay," she replied, "I just need a minute."

"Everyone, go back to sleep," Bridgot said, "I've got this."

They all tried to settle back down, obviously still unsure.

"What happened this time?" Bridgot asked, wrapping his arm around her and pulling her close.

"The same thing," she said, "Only this time, he also morphed into me, and each of you. And, instead of just making all of you disappear, he killed you."

Bridgot sighed, and she could hear the worry in it. Part of it was worry for her sake, but mostly, it was worry for the quest ahead. They all knew dreams were meant to tell you something.

What does it mean? she thought, *What could this dream be trying to tell me?*

Celestia tried to talk to a few of the other soldiers, but the results were the same. None of them cared about right and wrong. It didn't matter to any of them that the world could be plunged into darkness. They cared only about the orders of their commanders, the power of Zandor, and returning home to their families.

I must try the commanders, she thought, but none of them went on guard duty. They had more pressing matters to attend to. *The only way out of this is if they let us out,* she thought.

Days went by, and they were still stuck in the cage. Guards brought them food and water and made sure they didn't leave. They spent their time staring through the cage bars, dreaming of escape. There was nothing to do, and they were bored out of their minds.

Finally, one of the commanders came to the cage.

"Sir," the guard said, rising and saluting him.

Celestia and her warriors stirred, observing the situation with interest.

He was a tall man with brown hair and brown eyes, and a stern expression. He strode past the guard, right up to the cage. "Have you enjoyed your time with us?" he asked sarcastically.

"Let's see," Kgansten said, matching his sarcasm, "Your food is trash, your people are trash, and this cage is acutely uncomfortable. Overall, I'd have to say . . . no. Not really."

"Kgansten," Celestia whispered sharply.

The commander gave a sideways grin, "If you would like to be freed from your situation, I suggest you hand over the orb. We have nothing but time. There's no rush . . . for us."

"Well, if you know that we have a time crunch," Celestia said, "Then, you know what our mission is. Therefore, you know that we will not lightly abandon it."

He sneered, "So be it. Enjoy your time rotting in this cage. There will be no more meals. When you die, we will simply take the orb. The choice is yours. We care not for any of you. Our mission is to take the orb to Zandor. We don't have to kill you. But, we will."

As he turned to walk away, Celestia said, "Can I ask you a question?"

"What are you doing?" Bridgot whispered.

"Let me guess," he said, turning on his heel, "The same thing you've been asking my guards every night and day during their shifts? They all fear your silver tongue."

"Why should you fear it?" she asked, "You're a commander, not a soldier."

He smirked, "Alright. I'll play along. What is it you would ask of me?"

"My question is: Why? Why do you serve Zandor? What could you possibly gain?"

"Immunity," he said, "If we serve him, our countries will not be invaded by darkness. He's powerful enough to destroy us. Our families take priority."

"So, you care not for the rest of the world?" she asked in disbelief.

"The rest of the world is not our problem," he replied.

"I see," she said, "So, your motivations are completely selfish."

"No," he said, "They are for the good of our people. There's a large population in Mashang, Kogatsa, and Kuttub. They need to be protected."

"But, without you, he would have no army at his disposal. He may be powerful, but he is not invincible. Without an army, he could not take over. Without an army, *all* the lands of this world would be protected."

"We are the closest lands to him. He single-handedly destroyed the kingdom of Khanjgi and left its people defenseless. We are at the greatest risk. I will not sacrifice our people while we wait for some pitiful 'saviors' to complete a futile quest. I take our salvation where I can get it," he said forcefully.

"The armies of Mashang destroyed Khanjgi," she said, "He only showed up afterward, while the survivors were in hiding, already defenseless."

"How do you think he recruited the armies of Mashang?" he asked, "Think, princess."

"That's *queen*," she replied.

"It doesn't matter," he said, "Anyone who challenges him will die, including you."

Celestia looked him in the eyes then, "I do not fear him. I do not fear you. I do not fear death. I fear only for the world he would create, and what that would mean for all the people I care about, and even the people I don't." She looked at him pointedly.

"You may not fear death," he said, "But, death is coming to you either way." With that, he turned and walked away.

The next couple of days were hard, as they sat in the cage waiting, unable to do anything. They were not starving, however, as Celestia and Thaandor could use magic to produce food. It was almost too easy to thwart their captors' plan. Even if her wand and his staff were taken, they could still use their powers. Non-magical beings never fully understood how magic works.

While they sat in the cell, a star fell. They saw it through the skylight in the tunnels, and felt the shockwave from the explosion, as it landed outside. "We're running out of time," Celestia said, "There's only one star left. We have to get out of here."

"We'll never make it to Khanjgi in time," Thaandor said hopelessly.

"Don't think that way," Celestia said, "There must be a way."

While they tried to come up with a plan, the commanders began to get suspicious of them. They noticed they were not withering away, or begging for scraps, and they knew they were not starving like they wanted. They had the guards watch them closely, to ensure they were not somehow eating. In response, they stopped producing food so they wouldn't realize they could still wield magic.

As time wore on, and they began to actually starve, the commander returned, "Are you ready to give up the orb, yet?"

"You should already know the answer," Celestia said, "None of your forms of torture will make us give up. We're as dedicated to our side as you are to yours."

"Very well, then," he said, "You leave us no choice." He nodded to the guards, who opened the cage. The soldiers gathered before them, swords drawn.

"Finally!" Kgansten yelled, grabbing his axe from where their captors had stupidly left their weapons, right behind their cage.

Celestia, Bridgot, and Xharia grabbed their swords as well, readying themselves.

Thaandor used his magic to summon his staff, bringing it down, and blasting them back.

They began fighting once more, killing off more of the soldiers.

In response, the soldiers broke into groups, converging on each of them. Celestia realized they were trying to separate her and her warriors. *They must know I need all of them to complete the quest,* she thought, *At this rate, they'll get the orb from us. I have to do something.*

There were too many of them, though, and the group she was fighting was enough to engage her fully, driving her away from the rest of them. As she watched, they backed Bridgot into a corner, Xharia back into the cage, and Kgansten into a wall. She and Thaandor were being cornered as well, and she knew they couldn't hold them off.

"Hey, *queen*," the commander said suddenly, "How does it feel to know you failed? How does it feel to know you will never get the orb to Khanjgi to destroy it? How does it feel to know that you're about to watch your warriors die, one by one, and it's all your fault for leading them here?" With that, he drew his own sword, walking toward Bridgot. The soldiers had him pinned against the wall, and he couldn't escape.

"No!" she screamed. At that moment, something happened. She couldn't explain it, but something within her snapped, and she could feel her raw powers coursing through her. She waved her wand, putting a magical barrier around Bridgot right as the sword came down.

The commander looked back in anger at her, realizing she was responsible for saving Bridgot. When he saw her aglow with power, his jaw dropped. His sword fell from his hand, and he stood staring at her.

Celestia let her powers surge through her, feeling the tingling sensation that coursed through her veins. When the commander finally found his bearings, shouting for the soldiers to attack, she was ready. With a wave of her hand, she knocked them back. As they all tried to converge on her, she blasted them away, causing a shockwave almost as great as that of the falling stars.

The eyes of her warriors were as wide as the eyes of the soldiers, but she didn't care. She knew in that moment that she had the power to save their lives, and fulfill this quest. She cast a barrier around herself, walking forward confidently. None of the soldiers were able to touch her. As they tried to kill her warriors, she cast barriers around each of them, keeping them safe. The soldiers were unable to do anything but stop and stare as she walked to each warrior, bringing them with her.

When all five of them were together, she walked to the horse corral, and they all grabbed their horses. She scanned the faces of the fighters around her, glaring at the commander, "You've made a big mistake. It is not I who chose the losing side, but all of you. You will not hurt my warriors!"

As she yelled, she felt herself casting a spell, but she wasn't fully in control. She knew her emotions had gotten out of hand. They'd made her stronger and more vulnerable at the same time. She watched all the soldiers get blasted backward in an area the size of a crater. The faces of her warriors disappeared, and she felt like she was stuck in a windstorm, as the world went black.

The Last Star

14

Celestia looked around. She was sitting upon a grassy plain beside Razel. The fresh air was blowing through. Near her, Bridgot was beside Samson, his cape falling over his shoulders. Thaandor was beside Chevron, his hat falling off his gray-haired head. Kgansten was beside Gjabreel, his short legs in the air over his head. Xharia was beside Seina, her ebony face pressed to his leg, looking as though she might be sick.

Celestia felt drained, as if all her energy had been depleted. She collapsed in on herself, slumping against the ground, and pressing her face against the earth beneath her.

"Celestia!" Bridgot yelled, running over to her, "Are you alright?"

"I'm fine, Bridgot," she said, smirking at him, "You and your endless worrying."

"You and your knack for getting yourself into precarious situations," he retorted.

She smiled, her face still half smushed against the ground.

"Where are we?" Xharia asked, collecting herself.

Thaandor looked around, "We appear to be . . . " He gasped, darting from left to right as he tried to confirm what he was seeing. He looked back at them, "It can't be."

"What is it?" Bridgot asked.

"It's not possible."

"What's not possible?" Kgansten said, straightening himself up.

"It looks like we're . . . on the border between Kuttub and Kogatsa . . . "

"What?" Bridgot said, astounded.

Kgansten began darting from left to right, as Thaandor had done, trying to confirm their location.

"That's not possible," Xharia said.

"I know . . . " Thaandor agreed, still staring off into the distance.

Celestia felt weak and faint, sprawling out on the ground.

"Celestia!" Bridgot yelled again.

"She needs to rest," Thaandor said, rushing over, "If she just transported five people and their horses across the entirety of Kuttub, there's no telling how low her energy is."

Bridgot looked at her with concern.

"You and your endless worrying," Celestia whispered faintly.

He smiled weakly at her, grasping her hand.

Thaandor cast a spell to make the ground more comfortable for her, throwing a blanket on her to keep her warm. "I need to check her energy level," he said, hovering over her.

Kgansten and Xharia ventured closer, making sure she was okay.

Thaandor waved his staff over her, humming deeply and closing his eyes. After a few moments, he opened them, sitting back, "She'll be alright. She's not so low that her life is in danger. But, she does need to sleep. Now."

Bridgot stayed by her side, holding her hand and watching over her.

Thaandor ushered Xharia and Kgansten away, setting up their campsite, and putting up protective enchantments.

Celestia looked up at the sky, watching the puffy, white clouds sail across the bright blue expanse above her. For the first time in a long time, she felt like things would actually work out. She felt at peace as she drifted off to sleep.

When she woke, it was still daytime. Bridgot was no longer by her side. She slowly sat up, looking around.

"She's awake!" Kgansten yelled.

They all rushed to her side.

"Are you alright?" Bridgot asked.

"How are you feeling?" Xharia asked.

"Give her some space!" Thaandor yelled, pushing past them. After a pause, he said, "Do you feel restored?"

"I feel much better," she answered, "How is it still daylight? I feel like I've been asleep for a *while*."

Thaandor looked at the others, "You've been asleep for two days."

"Two days?" she yelled, "We can't afford to waste that kind of time! Why didn't anyone wake me?"

"You needed to recover your full strength," he answered, "You can't face Zandor on anything less."

"So, we haven't moved in two days?" she demanded.

"Do you know where we are?" Thaandor asked.

She looked around, "Not really."

"We are on the border of Kogatsa, a mere half day's ride from Khanjgi. We cannot go any closer until you are fully recovered."

"You mean that was real?" she said, "It wasn't a dream?"

"It wasn't a dream," Thaandor answered, "We're really here. *You* brought us."

"I thought you said it couldn't be done," Celestia countered.

He paused, looking at her, "It can't."

She looked around at the faces of her other warriors. Xharia's eyes picked up shades of brown and green, and even a bit of gold, as she stared at her in awe. Kgansten smiled through his rough, coarse beard at her. Bridgot gave her a knowing look, as though he understood and appreciated exactly what she could do.

As she looked at him, she said, "It was because of you."

"Because of me?" Bridgot asked, confused.

"Yes," she replied, "When the commander tried to kill you, something in me snapped. I had control of my powers as I shielded all of you, but I lost control, due to my heightened emotion, and that's how I managed to teleport us all here."

"Pure instinct," Thaandor said, amazed, "Your emotional reaction caused your powers to respond. Your mind was no longer in control, but your emotions. Your powers responded instinctually, without the need for spells."

"Isn't that dangerous?" Xharia asked.

"Extremely," Thaandor replied, "When your emotions reach such a peak that you lose control, anything could happen. It's like when you get so angry, you say things you don't mean, or do things you wouldn't normally do. Or, when you're so lost in grief, you lose control. When you have powers, particularly of Celestia's level, it's a bit different when we lose control of ourselves. But, it's the same concept—just with greater consequences."

Everyone looked back at Celestia again, "In that case, I just have one thing to say."

The four of them stared at her intently, waiting to hear what that one thing was.

"When I face Zandor, stay out of the way."

The rest of the day, Thaandor forced Celestia to eat and relax, ensuring her strength was completely recovered.

"We'll set out in the morning," he said.

"We're going to need a plan," Bridgot said.

"Yes, we are," Thaandor agreed.

"I'll go in first," Celestia said, "I have to face Zandor alone. Once he's defeated, bring the orb in, and we'll destroy it. We can only hope we succeed before the last star falls."

"No," Bridgot said, "You can't go in alone. I'll not wait outside for you like a coward."

"Bridgot," she said softly, "You can't face him. You don't have magic. Even Thaandor couldn't hope to match him. I have to do this."

"I agree," Thaandor inserted, "with Bridgot. You can't go in alone. We may not be able to face him for you, but we can distract him. Plus, it will give you strength and motivation. Your powers feed off of your emotions. You'd likely have stronger impulses if you believed we were in danger, particularly Bridgot."

"No," she said, "No way. I'll not use my husband as bait to increase my powers."

"I hate to do that to you," Thaandor said, "Believe me, I'd never want to put any of us in danger. But, it may be the only way to defeat him."

"He's right," Bridgot agreed, "It's the only way."

"I refuse to believe that," Celestia snapped, "It's not the only way. I can face him. I'm ready."

"You have powers the likes of which I could never hope to match," Thaandor said, "But, you're wrong. You're as prepared as I could make you, but you're not ready."

"Let me try first," she said, "And, if I look like I'm going to fail, then . . . go with your plan."

"We can't risk it," he replied, "There's too much at stake."

"I know what's at stake," she said, "We all do. But, I feel this is what I must do."

Thaandor shook his head.

"Celestia," Bridgot said, "Let me do this. I'm supposed to be your warrior. I'm supposed to protect you, and help you fulfill the prophecy. Yet, all this time, I've felt completely useless. I can fight with a sword, and I have basic archery skills, but I'm no better than your other warriors, or even you. I want to *do* something. I want to fulfill my role in all this. I want to bring something to the table that no one else could."

She looked at him lovingly, "You already have. Without you, I never could have gotten this far. You've saved my life several times. Ever since the day we met, you've been watching my back. You've done what you were supposed to do. No one else could have gotten me this far. It's my love for you—for the family we made together—that I keep going, and keep fighting."

"I don't want to be the guy who *married* to become king," he said, "I want to be the guy who *earned* his place as king."

She sighed, looking down. After a pause, she nodded, "Very well."

When she got up to take her shift, she felt worlds better. She had her full strength back, and she was ready to face Zandor. She stood leaning against Razel, watching over her sleeping warriors. Her eyes settled upon Bridgot. As she gazed upon the vulnerable innocence of his sleeping face, she smiled. He was everything to her, and she knew she could never bear to lose him. The more she thought about it, the more determined she became.

Finally, she leaped upon Razel's back, riding toward Khanjgi. Whatever happened, her warriors came first. She wouldn't lose them this time around. She knew in her heart she had to face Zandor alone. She took a breath, gritting her teeth as she rode. She never wanted to be part of any prophecy, but since she was, she was going to be the one to fulfill it.

Before mid-day, she made it to Khanjgi. She rode through the front gate, heading straight for the castle. The sun was hot overhead, and sweat began to drip down her pale face. When she reached the front entrance, she left Razel outside, pushing open the doors, and walking in.

Up the stairs she went, straight to the ritual room. Inside, Zandor was waiting, seated in a makeshift throne. He looked just as evil and ominous as she remembered. "Welcome, princess," he said, "I've been expecting you."

The ritual objects had finally been moved from the ground, and the table picked up. The room was even darker than she remembered, and the throne took up the whole back wall. The shadows danced with dark magic. She moved all the way into the room, inconspicuously grasping her wand from the folds of her dress.

"What? No army?" he chided, waving his arm, "I'm disappointed."

Celestia stared at him steadily.

"Not talking?" he asked, smirking. He paused, and his eyes moved to her hand, where she held her wand, "Straight to the fight, then."

She braced herself, holding his dark gaze.

He rose from his throne, drawing his own wand and quickly casting a curse her direction. She reacted swiftly, throwing up her barrier to protect herself. They exchanged a few blasts, knocking objects around the room.

He paused, looking at her, "Why are we wasting time?" With that, he summoned his dark magic to him, raw power exploding around him.

Celestia did the same, waiting with her wand drawn. She was ready to read her opponent, feeling her magic coursing through her. He launched another attack her way, and she blocked it, engaging him. It was nothing like facing Thaandor. She had expected the fight to be similar, but Zandor was much harder to read. He reacted quickly when she launched attacks at him, blocking nearly everything. He fired rapidly, and his attacks were much more powerful.

She struggled to match his speed, and it reminded her of when she'd first faced a real opponent after her sword training was complete. The only problem was that the first opponent she'd faced then had been easy to defeat, which was the perfect test of her skill. Zandor was her first real opponent, now that her magical training was complete. And, he was anything but easy to defeat.

Her energy began to wane as they went round and round, blasting through the bookshelves and ritual objects. She was determined to win, and she kept trying, blocking his curses and shooting blasts from her wand. As the fight wore on, he started to break down her barrier, and he could see he was gaining the upper hand. He summoned more power to himself, pulling from the darkness around him, and launched it at her, blasting her back into the wall.

"And to think," he said, "my mentor, the great Nazirdok, was so easily thwarted by you. You hadn't even discovered your powers yet. You were nothing. The world sings your praises for destroying him, but all you did was flip a table."

Celestia struggled to get up, feeling the drain of her stamina.

Zandor kicked her, knocking the wind out of her, "Don't get up. It's not necessary to rise in my presence. As I was saying, he should not have been defeated by the likes of you. He was too strong for that. He was focused on his ritual and didn't pay enough attention to his surroundings. He should have killed all of you when he had the chance. Believe me, I won't make the same mistake."

Her eyes widened as she watched him gather his energy to launch another attack at her.

Just then, Thaandor burst through the door, knocking Zandor across the room. Bridgot, Xharia, and Kgansten were right behind him, weapons drawn.

"Guards!" Zandor yelled, rising to his feet angrily.

Four tall, burly men in armor came marching through the door.

Celestia and her warriors looked at each other. Kgansten, Bridgot, and Xharia yelled, swinging axe and sword at the guards, and engaging them. Thaandor helped Celestia up, standing by her side to face Zandor.

He grinned, relishing the challenge, "So, old man, you dare to confront me?"

"I do not face you alone," he replied, "and nor does she."

Zandor laughed, "It matters not. Even combined, you're no threat to me."

"We'll see," he said. With that, Thaandor waved his staff, knocking Zandor back. He got up, launching an attack at them. Celestia joined her power with Thaandor's, blocking the spell. The battle began again, as they cast curse after counter-curse.

The guards proved a challenge for her other three warriors, as their battle wore on as well. At first, it seemed they were evenly matched, neither side able to gain the upper hand. But, as the fight wore on, Zandor and his guards started to dominate. Celestia wondered how they kept up their energy as they fought. She and her warriors' stamina was waning steadily.

Soon, she realized where their strength was coming from. She caught sight of Zandor, pulling energy from the darkness in the room. It was a cloud of strength, and she realized that he had stores of energy in the very air from which he could draw. *So, Nazirdok* did *teach him,* she thought.

The sky began to grow dark as they fought, and she knew the stars would be out soon. Something inside told her this night would be when the last star would fall. She struggled against Zandor, trying to get past his strength. It was no use. There was no telling how great his energy store was. For all she knew, he had the leftover stores of Nazirdok at his disposal.

Suddenly, it seemed as if her warriors had the upper hand, as Xharia leaped upon one of the guards, slitting his throat. Bridgot ran his sword through another. Kgansten brought his axe down upon a third. But, the fourth guard saw his opportunity, while they were focused on the other three, and he grabbed Kgansten, bringing his sword forward to meet him.

Celestia threw her barrier over to him, saving his life. The point of the sword still stuck him, though, since it took a second for the barrier to reach him. He fell, and Bridgot grabbed him, pulling him to the side as Xharia killed the final guard.

When Celestia projected her barrier, she left herself open, and Zandor took his opportunity. He blasted her and Thaandor with everything he had, breaking Thaandor's barrier easily, and knocking them back. Thaandor was knocked unconscious, and a single line of blood began to stream from his head. Celestia felt her own stamina completely depleted, and she knew she had no energy left to keep fighting.

Zandor pinned her warriors to the wall with tentacles of dark magic, seeing he had won. He grinned, walking up to her, "How does it feel, knowing you'll never be able to beat me, and that you'll never be able to protect your . . . family?"

"What . . . do you mean by that?" she asked breathlessly.

"I was hoping you'd ask," he said, "Why don't you call your mother?"

Celestia sucked in a breath of surprise, panicking. Thoughts of her family raced through her mind like wildfire. She summoned a pool of water, calling her mother on it.

"Celestia?" her mother said, looking and sounding panicked.

"Mom!" she yelled, "Are you alright?"

Distracted, she could hear her mother yelling, "Natasha, take the kids and go! Get out of here!"

She watched with horror as Natasha and the kids ran away in the background, and she heard their screams of fright. There were soldiers there, and the safe-house was on fire. She saw her mother draw a sword, a look of determination on her face.

"Mom!" she yelled again.

Her mother dropped the witch's glass as she swung the sword, engaging the soldiers. When the glass hit the ground, the connection was lost. She looked up at Zandor furiously, "What have you done?"

He laughed, "Ensured my victory. Now, hand over the orb, or let your mother and children die."

Her eyes widened in horror, and she looked at her warriors. They looked back at her, and she locked eyes with Bridgot. She saw a tear stream down his face as he shook his head, "You can't give it to him, Celestia . . . even for our children." He sucked in a breath, "This is our destiny. This is our curse."

"You should listen to your husband," Zandor said, "This is the last time you two will speak, after all."

She looked back at him as a terrible realization hit her, "It doesn't matter if I give you the orb or not. You're not going to stop the soldiers. You're going to try to kill my family anyway."

His smirk turned to a look of irritation as he realized she wasn't going to give him the orb, "Not try. They *will* be killed." With that, he summoned one final blast of dark magic to him.

Celestia felt her rage build up inside her, and the pure fear for the lives of her children and her mother. Her body glowed with intensity, and she let out a yell, power exploding from her. Zandor's blast had no effect, and he was thrown across the room. He stood up, surprised, as he looked at her glowing form. Fear flickered across his face.

She tapped into the energy in her ring to sustain her, as her body was completely worn. She felt refreshed instantly, allowing strength to flow through her freely. Zandor gathered his powers to him again, pulling energy from the darkness, but she could see he was afraid. She had him right where she wanted him. She waited for him to blast her again, and she launched her magic at the blast, dissipating it. She smiled, knowing she now had the upper hand.

Celestia began her counter-attack, hitting him with an onslaught of blasts, and wearing him down steadily. She backed him into his throne, preparing for her final attack. When he fell against it, unable to defend himself against her might, she summoned the full force of her powers, and, with a flash of light brighter than all the stars combined, blasted Zandor with it.

When the light cleared, Zandor was gone, and all that was left of him was a pile of charred rubble. She breathed a sigh of relief, looking back at her warriors. Thaandor was regaining consciousness, and Xharia was by his side, helping him sit up slowly. Bridgot was beside Kgansten, looking at him worriedly.

"Quickly!" she shouted, "We must destroy the orb!"

Bridgot unwrapped it, placing it in the middle of the floor. He helped Kgansten to his feet, handing him the axe of Kgoresh the Terrible. He grabbed the sword of Vidar the Conqueror, bracing himself. Xharia snatched up Aurano's bow and quiver, and Thaandor pulled out the wand of Merlin.

They stood around the orb, and Thaandor cast the spell over it, il-luminating it in silver magic. As soon as he did, they caught sight of the last star, falling from the sky. Celestia started running over, and Kgansten brought the axe down upon it, cracking its surface. Xharia shot an arrow at it, and it stuck up, out of the crack. Bridgot swung the sword down on it, deepening the fissure. Celestia reached Ezmyra's talon, leaping to the orb, and plunging it into it right as the star hit the ground outside, sending a shockwave through the castle, and shaking its foundation. There was an ominous pause as they waited to see if they had been successful. Finally, the crack traveled down the orb, and it shattered, releasing the powers within.

"Oh, no!" Celestia shouted, "We're too late!"

The darkness raised up into a cloud, and from it, stepped Nazirdok.

Celestia's eyes widened as she looked at him, and he grinned at her, stepping forward. The moment his foot touched the floor, there was a hiss-ing sound, as it began to burn. He screeched, smoke coming from his foot. The heat traveled up his leg, and they watched as he began to bubble and steam, as though he had lava inside him. His screams of agony pierced the night as he finally exploded, and steaming liquid burst around the room.

Celestia and her warriors ducked, avoiding the splash. Moonlight streamed in through the skylight, and his remains were evaporated, along with the darkness, up and away, leaving the room bright and peaceful, the heavy feeling of dark magic gone.

She dropped to her knees, feeling relief and exhaustion sweeping through her. As she looked around at her warriors, she realized how heavy a toll this quest had taken. Thaandor was using his remaining energy to heal the wound on his head. Bridgot and Xharia looked weary. Kgansten was clutching the sword wound as it bled into his hand.

Celestia crawled over to him, placing her hand upon the wound.

"No," Thaandor said, "Your energy is too low."

"So is yours," she replied, "If I don't, he'll die." With that, she concentrated, picturing how the wound was supposed to be, "*Shuleas.*" Her blue magic radiated from her hand, and the wound sealed itself up, the skin reattaching.

"Thank you," Kgansten said.

Celestia nodded, lying down on the floor and blacking out.

A Hundred Years

15

As sunlight streamed in through the skylight, Celestia sat up. She looked around the room and saw her warriors beginning to regain consciousness, too. She guessed they had all been exhausted from the fight as well, and had needed to rest, same as her. They all looked much better. Thaandor's head was healed, with dried blood sticking to his face. Kgansten held his back as he stood, still fully recovering from his stab wound. Bridgot and Xharia looked well-rested. Celestia let out a sigh of relief that they were all okay.

"Is everyone alright?" Bridgot asked.

They all nodded and mumbled a few *yeses* his direction.

Celestia crossed to his side, hugging him.

He paused in surprise, but wrapped his arms around her.

"Thank you," she said.

"For what?" he asked.

"For fulfilling your part in this quest. You've saved my life many times. You saved Kgansten, too. You've fought countless battles, and pulled your weight. You may not feel like you've done much, but you've contributed more than you know," she said, "It was you who decided to journey to see The Oracle, in order to stop the war in our land and save our people. You thought of them, and thought of your duty first, as any ruler should. You have truly *earned* your place as king."

He gave her a half-smile, "Even though I didn't have the power to defeat Zandor for you, it's good to know I did my part. And, even though you went in first like we told you not to, it's good to know my wife can defend herself. It takes some of my worry from me, knowing I don't *always* have to watch your back."

She smiled, "I'm sorry I didn't listen. You all are my first priority. You're all family to me. I didn't want anything to happen to you—to any of you. I didn't want to put you in harm's way just for motivation. But, I was wrong. It was better you than our children."

"No," he said, "You were right. It was better that you got there first. Everything happened the way it did for a reason. The timing was perfect. We did it."

She smiled again, "Yes. *We* did."

"Let's get these weapons back where they belong," Thaandor said, "I'm not interested in having the wizard council pursuing us for stealing the wand of Merlin."

Celestia laughed, "Me, neither."

They walked outside, getting their horses, and riding out of Khanjgi. The sun was shining, and the town no longer looked dark and ominous, but bright and peaceful, without the threat of dark magic looming over it.

When they were out of the city, Xharia said, "I'll take the dwarven, elven, and human weapons south. I have to go that way anyway, to return home. And, it will keep all of you safe from my father. I'll try to talk to him for you, and convince him to pardon you."

"Thank you," Bridgot said, "But, we can't let you go alone."

"I'll go with her," Kgansten inserted, "My home is south as well. Call my family and tell them to make the journey home without me. I'll meet them there. Since the prophecy is fulfilled and the world is at peace, it should be safe for them to make the trip, now."

Bridgot nodded, "I'll send two of our guards with them, to ensure they make it safely."

"Thank you," Kgansten said.

They dismounted their horses, embracing. The remaining warriors did the same, as they said their *goodbyes*.

"Journey south together," Bridgot said, "Kgansten, take the axe of Kgoresh the Terrible to your uncle, and make things right in the kingdom of Dirthix. Xharia, you can journey from there alone, to Garellis, and return Aurano's bow and arrow to your people. Hopefully, you can reconcile things with your father, and we can still count the elves as our friends."

"I hope so, too," she said, "But, even if I can't, you can always count *me* as your friend."

Bridgot and Celestia nodded, smiling, and Celestia reached out to hug Xharia.

"What of the sword of Vidar the Conqueror?" she asked.

"We'll take that with us," Bridgot replied, "They are no longer my village. I am not obligated to bring anything to them. And with a weasel like Elder Carsen in charge, they don't deserve such a historic weapon. It should be displayed in a true museum of human weapons, not locked away in a weapons depository. Something tells me he won't be trying to fight me on that."

"How do you know?" Xharia asked.

"The prophecy is fulfilled. We are to enjoy a hundred years of peace, with no wars. To challenge my decision would mean open war. Therefore, I know he won't. That, and he's a cowardly snake."

Xharia nodded, "Very well. Goodbye, all of you."

They all embraced again, saying their final *goodbyes* to Xharia and Kgansten. As the dark elven beauty and the red-bearded dwarf rode south upon their steeds, Celestia smiled to Bridgot. Though she would miss them, she knew it was only goodbye for now, not forever. The three of them rode west, heading across Mashang, toward Abyumo, and the realm of the wizards.

When they stopped to make camp that night, Celestia pooled some water before her, taking a breath, and calling up her mother. Natasha answered, and the picture was cracked, which Celestia was sure was from when her mother had dropped it.

"Celestia?" she said, staring into the broken witch's glass.

Her heart sank with worry upon seeing Natasha's face on the surface of the water, "Natasha?"

"Did you do it?" she asked.

"Yes," Celestia answered, "We did it. The quest is complete. There will be no more wars, and the land will know peace for the next hundred years."

Natasha breathed a sigh of relief, "Then it's safe to return to the castle?"

"Yes," she said, "It's safe. Are my children with you? Are they alright?"

"They're perfectly fine," Natasha answered, tilting the mirror so Celestia could see her son and daughter, huddled together with Kganley, Kganzar, and Nedebarth.

It was Celestia's turn to breathe a sigh of relief, "What about my mother?"

Natasha looked away, "I'm not sure. I took the kids and left the safe-house. Soldiers came. They found us and lit it on fire. Your mother held them off so I could get the children to safety. One of your servants took us in and sheltered us. We're at her house now. I wasn't sure if we could go back to the castle yet. I went to the safe-house yesterday, and your mother wasn't there. I found the mirror you gave her to talk to you with, and I hoped we'd get a call from you sooner or later."

She sucked in a breath, "Okay. Take the kids and go back to the castle. Bring the servants with you. Let them know it's safe. Which one are you with?"

"She says her name's Garrita," Natasha answered.

Celestia smiled, "Of course it is. Okay, Kgansten is on his way back home, to Korga. He wants you and the boys to meet him there. Bridgot has issued the order for two of our guards to escort you. After you get everyone back to the castle, you can take them and go. Leave the children with Garrita. They'll be safe with her. If you find my mother, give the witch's glass to her. Otherwise, leave that with Garrita, too."

Natasha nodded, "I will."

"Thank you," Celestia said.

"No," Natasha replied, "Thank you."

With that, they severed the connection, and Celestia went to sleep with a knot of worry in her stomach. *Be alright, mom,* she thought, *Please be alright.*

Bridgot, Celestia, and Thaandor journeyed through Mashang quickly, as it was still unoccupied, and made their way into Fluorasti. It only took a week and a half, much like the journey there. Fluorasti would take a fortnight to cross. As they moved through, Thaandor continued to train Celestia in the ways of magic.

"I know you won't need to fight anymore," he said, "But I can teach you convenience spells that are good to know. It can only benefit you to possess further knowledge of what you're doing."

"I suppose you're right," Celestia said, "Despite what The Oracle says, I guess we never really know what the future will hold."

"You should come to the wizard realm," Thaandor prodded, "to complete your training fully."

"No," she said, "I have to fulfill my duties as queen. Not to mention," she looked at Bridgot, "I have a family to think of."

"Very well," he sighed, "I suppose I should have known."

He taught her many useful spells that she could use around the castle, some of which would even help restore the damage that had been done to it by the soldiers. Celestia knew she would miss her mentor when they said *goodbye*, but she also knew she would miss her family more. She belonged in Ivétoiless.

She learned how to set protective enchantments, and was able to put them around their campsite at night. She learned how to mend broken objects, how to lift things with magic, and how to form the ground (creating hills, valleys, or plains at will).

The two-week journey flew by, as they made their way through Fluorasti without making any stops. Though they were certain the villages would be less hostile this time around, as the quest was complete, the world was at peace, and they were no longer in danger, they didn't want to take the extra time. It had been about five months since they'd departed, and they knew the journey to the wizard realm was at least three weeks. They didn't want to risk any delays in returning the wand of Merlin.

The whole way, Celestia was worried for her mother, and eager to see her children. She missed them all terribly, and she was glad their quest was finally over. Though she had enjoyed the adventure, the escape from the mundane, and the time away with her husband, she was homesick, and she knew she would not miss the danger, or the weight of the world on her shoulders.

When they reached Cardeas, Celestia began to hope they'd run into Nastazya's brothers again. She wanted to know they were alright, and that they had made it through Cardeas' war with Gachichken. They made camp in a secluded clearing, and she realized it was the very same clearing they had camped in after the battle they'd fought with the brothers. The ravine was across from them, and they were right on the border between Cardeas and Fluorasti.

"It will take us another week to get through Cardeas, and make it to The Wizarding Museum in Abyumo," Thaandor said.

"Yes," Bridgot agreed, "We shall arrive with time to spare to return the wand."

"I certainly hope so," he replied, "I can't relax until I know it's been returned successfully."

"I transported five people and their horses across Kuttub," Celestia said, "If need be, I can transport three the rest of the way to Abyumo."

"You had strong enough emotion then," Thaandor countered, "Without it, I'm afraid the spell would truly be impossible."

"I hope I don't have cause for such great emotion again," she replied, "Regular emotions are good enough for me."

"I always thought you wanted something more," he said, "But, I see now that you are content with the life of a royal."

"My adventurous spirit has not died," she said, "It is simply satisfied. I know my place and my duty to my people and my family. That is where my heart is. I've had my fill of adventure for the next hundred years after that one. I'm happy with what I have, and I'm ready to go home."

"Me, too," Bridgot said, "I thought I wanted a life of adventure, but really, I just needed another quest to quench my thirst. I thought we'd lost something after our last quest, but we didn't. It was simply suppressed for the time being. I thought life was boring and mundane, but I've grown to appreciate the peace of everyday life. We've fought hard enough for it. We've earned it. I think I'll be satisfied for the next hundred years as well."

Celestia smiled, "Glad to hear it."

He grasped her hand, "No matter how routine our life becomes, I don't think I could ever be bored with you."

Thaandor sighed.

"Have you never known love, Thaandor?" Celestia asked.

He looked at her, "Once. Her name was Theodora. She was a beautiful witch, even as her hair turned silver with age. But, alas, it was not to be. For, she didn't love me back. She was in love with another. When she moved north, I vowed I would never love again. When I got news of her passing, I . . . " He looked away.

"I'm sorry," she said, taking his hand.

"Wizards accomplish more on their own, anyway," he said softly, still looking away.

"Maybe so," she replied, "But, no one deserves to be lonely."

"I'm not alone," he said, "I have many friends around me. The Oracle and I keep each other company, and I know several wizards and dragon riders I can visit whenever I wish. I've lived a long time, and so have they. Some of them even knew her. I don't need romantic companionship in light of so many friendships."

"You know," she said softly, "Just because one relationship didn't work doesn't mean you're condemned to never have one."

"I know," he said, patting her hand, "But, that's the only one I've ever wanted."

She gave him a half-smile, sitting beside him wordlessly. Bridgot sat on the other side, and they stared up into the starry sky, and the dark line of empty space where seven stars used to be.

Weapons Return

16

"The princess has returned!" Jacobi shouted in greeting on seeing Bridgot, Celestia, and Thaandor riding up.

"Jacobi," she said, dismounting to hug him, "Chiumbo, Thabiti, Theodonis, Ajala."

They each nodded to her, hugging her in turn.

"Great to see you all," she said, "I was worried for you."

"No reason to worry for us," Ajala said, "We told you we are Cardeas' greatest warriors. It is the other side who should fear us."

"What happened?" Bridgot asked, standing beside his wife.

"Our leaders reached a truce," Jacobi answered, "It seems Gachichken thought it fair to grant us a share of land, as they have so much of it already, and hardly anyone resides in the northern part."

Celestia smiled, shaking her head in disbelief. *The Oracle was right, after all*, she thought, *The lands of this world are at peace.*

"You look weary from your travels," Thabiti said, "Why don't you stay with us tonight?"

"Thank you," Celestia said, "We would love that."

"Wonderful," Jacobi replied, "Come on in."

The three of them followed the brothers inside, as they led them down the hall to the spare rooms.

"What happened to your dwarf friend?" Chiumbo asked.

"He returned home to his people," Bridgot answered, "along with our elf friend we gained along the way. You didn't have the chance to meet her, but she was friends with Aurano and daughter of the elf king."

Chiumbo nodded, "I see."

"We shall prepare a hot meal for you all tonight," Theodonis said, "I'm sure you could use one."

"Yes, we could," Celestia agreed, "Thank you again."

He gave her a nod.

"We'll leave you to wash up," Thabiti said.

With that, the brothers disappeared down the hall to the kitchen, leaving the three of them standing in the hallway. It was just as Celestia remembered: a small, simple house, made of oak, with lots of bedrooms, a kitchen, two bathrooms, a living area, and an underground hideout. Their decorations were colorful, livening up the otherwise plain house.

The three of them took turns washing up, and by the time they were done, the brothers had dinner ready. They followed their noses to the kitchen, where the five of them were serving up a meal of meat and potatoes.

"Dinner is served," Ajala said, setting the last dish on the table.

"Smells delicious," Celestia said.

"Thank you for your hospitality," Thaandor added.

"Of course," Jacobi said, "A friend of our sister's is a friend of ours."

They all sat down to eat, enjoying the food, talking and laughing with Nastazya's brothers. It felt like home to Celestia, and, to her, they were family. It made her miss Nastazya, but she knew she would always miss her, and Aurano. She couldn't let herself get lost in grief, however. She could only keep their memory alive and honored, and live her own life to the fullest.

After dinner, they helped the brothers clean up, and Celestia thought she'd never had that much fun doing dishes before. They had a system for getting them done, with all five of them helping. Plates, cups, and silverware were flying all around, as Thabiti cleared the dishes from the table, tossing them to Jacobi and Ajala, who washed them in the sink, and tossed them to Theodonis and Chiumbo to dry and put away, tossing them in the cabinets, and stacking them effortlessly. After they saw how the system worked, the brothers had Bridgot and Thaandor clear the plates, while Celestia and Thabiti dried them, tossing them to Theodonis and Chiumbo to put away. They were almost disappointed when there were no more dishes to wash, as they were all laughing and enjoying themselves.

"Don't worry," Chiumbo said, "There's plenty of good company to go around."

The eight of them went outside, where they set up a bonfire, gathering around to tell stories.

Celestia and Bridgot told the story of their first quest, and Thaandor joined in to talk about the second. Then, Thaandor told the story of how he met The Oracle and began his life as her keeper. After that, it was the brothers' turn to tell a story.

"I'm not sure how we can top the adventures the three of you have had," Jacobi said, "But, we have had adventures of our own still worthy of sharing."

"Perhaps not as great as our sister," Thabiti said, "She was a legend of Cardeas, going from a poor peasant warrior to a dragon rider."

"She never saw as many battles as we did," Ajala inserted.

"For that, I'm grateful," Theodonis said, "She shouldn't have had to see as many battles as us."

"Instead of sharing our own stories of battle," Chiumbo said, "We should tell one of the stories of the Great Ones."

"Yes," Ajala agreed eagerly, "I'm sure they haven't heard them before."

"Very well," Jacobi said, silencing everyone, "The greatest of them all was Derekkian. He was native to Cardeas, and an often overlooked part of history by the rest of the world. He was a young peasant boy. Nobody knew his name. Until the world needed a hero . . . "

"The armies of Vidar the Conqueror had risen up," Theodonis continued, "They were unstoppable, taking over every kingdom of every land they pillaged through. As you may know, he had taken over 90% of the human realm. He thought himself invincible, and indeed, it seemed that way."

"Derekkian knew he had to be stopped," Chiumbo said, "But, he wasn't sure how to do it. So many great warriors had failed. How could he, a nameless peasant, do anything different?"

"But, he had a strategy up his sleeve," Ajala said, "He was more than he appeared. He had more heart than many soldiers he'd known, and he was determined to prove himself, and to save Cardeas from being taken over."

"He had many friends from other races," Thabiti continued, "He was a messenger for his kingdom, and he had been to the lands of the wizards and dragon riders many times. He'd even journeyed as far as the lands of the elves and the dwarves."

"All he had to do was get them on their side," Jacobi said, "and convince them to fight. His main dilemma was how he would get his own people to follow him, when, in their eyes, he was no one special. He was no soldier. He was no leader."

"So, he called first on his friends from outside the kingdom," Theodonis said, "He thought if he told them he had an army, and a plan, he could get them to join him."

"And, he was right," Chiumbo continued, "Once he got the armies of the wizards, dragon riders, elves, and dwarves to join him, he was able to convince his own people to follow him easily."

"Once he had a force amassed," Ajala said, "he knew he had a chance. He gathered soldiers and citizens from the occupied countries who longed to be part of a resistance effort against their conqueror. He started a race of warriors. He's the reason we have soldiers and warriors today, and that they're not the same thing. Warriors have heart, and they fight for what's right. Soldiers follow their leader, just doing their job."

I know that's true, Celestia thought.

"He led the resistance that finally defeated Vidar the Conqueror," Thabiti said, "A simple peasant boy from Cardeas orchestrated the largest counter-offensive in history. He restored freedom to the land, and proved people could fight for what they believe in."

"He also opened the doors for alliances with the other races," Jacobi finished, "If it weren't for the bravery and cunning of Derekkian, we might still be living under the influence of Vidar's descendants."

"Wow," Bridgot said, "I grew up on stories of Vidar the Conqueror, but I never knew who was responsible for the resistance that finally stopped him."

"Indeed," Theodonis said, "Most aren't."

"He really deserves more credit," he said.

"Yes, he does," Theodonis agreed.

"I hope you will help us spread his story across other lands," Jacobi said.

"You can count on it," Bridgot replied.

He smiled, "It's getting late. You all need a good night's sleep before you set out."

"Indeed we do," Thaandor agreed.

With that, they all filed into the house, going to their respective rooms, and getting comfortable. Lying in a bed for the first time since they left Kgansten's house, it was all too easy to drift off.

The next morning, they said their *goodbyes* to Nastazya's brothers, setting out for Abyumo. They journeyed all day, departing from Cardeas, and crossing the corner of Gachichken, which, as it turned out, was now part of Cardeas. When they stopped to make camp that night, enjoying the leftovers the brothers had packed for them, Thaandor said, "It will only take a couple of days to reach The Wizarding Museum and return the wand."

"Yes," Bridgot said, "And, with a few days to spare."

"Assuming all goes according to plan," he added.

"Nothing had better go wrong now," Celestia interjected, "We're supposed to be enjoying our hard-earned peace, and returning home."

"Indeed," Thaandor agreed, "I just like to be prepared, and leave room for the unknown."

"If there's anything else The Oracle neglected to mention, she can finish the quest herself," Celestia said.

Bridgot chuckled, "I second that."

"She said that was it," Thaandor said, "She wasn't wrong the first time. There were simply variables she had neglected. This time, she specifically said that was it. Therefore, we're in the clear."

"Then there's nothing to worry about," Celestia said.

They all continued eating their meat and potatoes, each of them eager to reach their journey's end, and return to their respective homes. The closer they got, the more anxious Celestia got to see her children and discover what happened to her mother. Thaandor had advised her not to use the witch's glass anymore, since it was broken. Broken witch's glasses could cause broken connections, which could drain a wizard's powers too low, and kill them. So, she had no way to contact any of them until she arrived. Thaandor gave her a new witch's glass that she could give to them upon her return, in case she needed it again at a future point. But, it didn't help ease her mind for the time being.

As much as she'd enjoyed their visit with Nastazya's brothers, now that they were back on the road, that was the only thing she could focus on: getting home. It occupied her thoughts as she drifted off to sleep that night, and she knew Bridgot and Thaandor were anxious to arrive as well. She hoped that Kgansten and Xharia had made it to Dirthix, and that Xharia was on her way home. She also hoped that Natasha and the boys had made it across Gachichken and into Korga. But, she had no way to contact them, as they did not possess magic powers. So, she could only hope.

The final thought that fluttered through her mind was the same thought she'd had every night since departing Kogatsa, *Please be alright, mother.*

They rode into Abyumo, in the realm of the wizards, and made their way to The Wizarding Museum. As they dismounted, walking up to the tall, glistening, gray stone building, Thaandor withdrew the wand of Merlin. The moment they stepped foot in the museum, looking up at the great, golden statue of Merlin, the wizard council appeared before them.

"We felt the presence of the wand," the head elder said.

"You have returned it in time," another added.

"Yes," Thaandor said, "Here it is."

He handed the wand to the council, who accepted it, bowing. They headed down the left-most corridor, to return it to its display case.

Thaandor breathed a sigh of relief, "We did it."

"That's it?" Celestia asked, "We just hand it to them and go?"

"What did you expect?" Thaandor said, "We won't be getting a parade for returning the wand of Merlin. We were lucky they let us borrow it in the first place. Yes, all we had to do was return it to the hands of the council. They're putting it back in its display, and all is well in the wizard realm. We're finished."

"We're not done quite yet," Bridgot said, "Come on."

The three of them set out from the museum, riding toward the dragon rider realm. It was a couple of days away, but they were nearing the end of their journey. They had only to return the talon of Ezmyra to the riders and speak with The Oracle before heading home.

The wizard realm was beautiful; lush with life, mountainous, and home to the exquisite phoenix—the most powerful of the elemental birds. Dirthens mostly spent their time burrowing through the dwarven tunnels, keeping to themselves. Dwervas and auristras swooped through the skies of the land of the elves. They were powerful, but not as much so as phoenixes. She was awed by the beauty of their flame-colored wings, and the glow they gave off as they flew overhead.

When they crossed into the desert plain of the dragon rider realm, they galloped eagerly across, reaching the gate to the great city in record time. The guards allowed them inside, and they went up to the castle, heading straight for Kirstiana's throne room. She was there, seated on her throne, in all her amber glory, but Solstra was nowhere to be found.

"Where is your dragon?" Celestia asked.

"Strange greeting," Kirstiana said, "But, I suppose it shows your concern for the great, ancient creatures. She is off hunting. Sometimes she enjoys flying around, getting fresh air and exercise, and finding her own food. Dragons can never fully be domesticated. Besides, she can't be expected to lie napping in the throne room *all* the time, can she?"

"No," Celestia said, "I suppose not."

"You have brought the talon back, I assume?"

"Yes," Thaandor answered, presenting it.

"Excellent," she said, "Then your quest was successful?"

"What do you care?" Bridgot asked, "You refused us a warrior when we came to you in our time of need."

"I granted you the weapon you needed, didn't I? I gave you an audience with the council. I can't be blamed for their decision. Part of being queen is acknowledging and accepting the will of the council. If I didn't take their opinions into consideration, I wouldn't be queen, now would I?"

"We were successful, indeed," Thaandor said.

"Yes," Celestia agreed, "Luckily, I was able to fill in for the missing warrior. I think I made a fine substitute for a dragon rider." She smirked, winking at Bridgot.

Kirstiana looked at her, twisting her lips. After a pause, she said, "Well, I'm glad you were able to save the world again. Hopefully, this time it will *stay* saved, and there won't be any other missing pieces to the prophecy."

"There won't be," Thaandor replied, "I have already spoken with The Oracle, and she has informed me that the prophecy is completely fulfilled."

"Excellent," she said, "Well, you all may stay here tonight, and set out at dawn. I thank you for returning the talon to us." She waved one of her servants over, who took the talon from Thaandor and scurried out of the throne room.

The three of them showed themselves to the guest suites, washing up and getting comfortable as Loretta brought them some food. They enjoyed the meal of smoked meat, charred vegetables, and fresh fruits from the fertile soil. All of the foods the dragon riders enjoyed were prepared with dragon fire, which made for a unique flavor they couldn't get anywhere else.

"It will be a pity to not have an excuse to visit the dragon riders again," Celestia said, "Their food is so wonderful."

"They are friends," Thaandor said, stuffing his mouth with fruit, "What excuse do you need? Just visit."

"They are friends to you," Bridgot retorted, "I'm not so sure they care for our company."

"Nonsense," he said, "Kirstiana likes the both of you, otherwise she would not let us stay here, or provide us with such an exquisite meal. I visit quite often, and I'm certain you would be welcome as well."

Bridgot looked at him doubtfully, exchanging a sideways glance with Celestia.

"I'm sure we shall make the occasion to visit," she said, "if for nothing else than to appreciate their cuisine."

Thaandor laughed, "It will be wonderful to see more of you; that's for certain."

When they'd finished their meal, they lied down to sleep, watching the dancing green fractals of light skate across the walls in the moonlight. *I wonder what The Oracle will have to say,* Celestia thought, *It's finally time for real answers . . .*

As the light of dawn shone through the walls of the glittering dragon rider castle, the three of them got their horses and set out across the desert plain of the dragon rider realm back toward the wizard realm. They passed through the barrier, going from dry, dusty desert to tall, green grass full of flowers. They made their way to the elliptical, ivory home of The Oracle.

"Go on in," Thaandor said, turning to Celestia, "The two of you have much to discuss."

Celestia went up the familiar stairs, and into the blinding light and strong wind of The Oracle's home. When the light died down enough for her to see The Oracle, she said, "Is it really over? There's not going to be some missing piece later on, is there?"

"It is over," she answered, "You have completely fulfilled the prophecy I foresaw, and there will be one hundred years of uninterrupted peace."

Celestia breathed a sigh of relief, the flowy blue skirt of her gown billowing around her softly. After a pause, she said, "I asked you a question last time I was here. Will you give me an answer now?"

The Oracle smiled, "I will. Everything in this world has an opposite; light and dark, day and night, moon and sun, ground and sky, plant and animal. So, every*one* has an opposite. You were able to thwart Nazirdok because *you* were his opposite. In every possible way, you were what he wasn't, and he was what you weren't. That is why you were the only one who could defeat him. No one else's power could have stopped him. He'd gathered too much energy. When you first receive your powers, you're at your strongest. He wasn't expecting anyone to be able to defeat him, least of all you. That's why he didn't take you seriously as a threat. His arrogance was his downfall. When you were able to break through his spell and stop his ritual, he was entirely unprepared for the possibility."

"I'm Nazirdok's opposite?" she asked.

"You're his downfall and his weakness," she said, "Everything must have balance. There can only be as much good as bad in this world, and vice versa. If the scales tip too much to either side, chaos is the result."

"So, I was born to balance the darkness he created," Celestia said.

It wasn't a question, but The Oracle responded, "Yes. But, after he was defeated, and his powers contained in the orb, you became the light wizard who possesses raw power. When a wizard of one side possesses the gift, there must be a wizard of the other side who also can, for balance."

"Zandor," Celestia whispered.

"Yes," she replied, "Zandor is Thaandor's opposite. When his mentor was killed, he gained the ability to wield raw power, to bring balance to light and dark. You and Thaandor are the opposite pairing of Zandor and Nazirdok, in every way."

"But, if we destroyed them, doesn't that mean the balance is off again?" she asked.

The Oracle smiled, "No. You don't plan on using your powers, so there isn't a force for good that must be balanced by evil. You killed your opposites, so now you don't have them. The two of you are living against nature. Eventually, it will catch up. But, not for quite a while."

"A hundred years?" Celestia asked.

She smiled again, "Indeed. Your opposites tipped the scales toward evil, with their plan to plunge the world into darkness. You and Thaandor tipped the scales toward good, with your strong moral compasses, and your powerful magic. I only saw that one of you would win. Forces of your magnitude cannot be contained. You cannot coexist together. One of you must defeat the other. That is how I knew that your victory or failure would mean the tipping of the scales for the next hundred years."

She was silent, contemplating everything.

"No more questions?" The Oracle asked, "Normally, you're full of them."

"Normally, I'm embarking on a quest, and I need to know what to do to succeed," she said, "Now, my quest is at an end, and I only needed to know how I was able to win. So, Zandor got his powers because of me. How is it I am able to wield raw powers?"

"Your opposite was too powerful. Though Nazirdok could not wield raw power, he had massive energy stores. You had to be born with the ability to combat that."

She was silent again. After a pause, she said, "So, what now?"

"That, Celestia," The Oracle said, "Is up to you."

Princess Nastazya

17

Celestia and Bridgot said their *goodbyes* with Thaandor, readying themselves for the journey home.

"We hope to see you again, often," Bridgot said, hugging him.

"I second that," Celestia said, giving him a hug after.

"I shall certainly come to see you both," Thaandor replied, "And, I should hope for you to visit me. I know my life isn't the most exciting, watching over The Oracle, but . . . "

"We'd love to visit," Celestia assured him.

Bridgot smiled, patting him on the back in agreement.

"Safe journey home," Thaandor said, "May you find your mother."

"Thank you, Thaandor," Celestia said, giving him a half-smile. She and Bridgot leaped upon Samson and Razel's backs, riding south for Duwazo.

It took a few days to reach it, but soon enough, their castle was in their sights. They could see that it was partially in ruins, with stones crumbling toward the ground, and a few of the rooms visible from the outside. The grounds were trampled and torn up, with dirt strewn everywhere. They made their way inside, seeing several of the servants trying to clean up and make repairs.

"Bridgot? Celestia?" Garrita said when she saw them, "Bridgot! Celestia!" She rushed over to embrace them.

"Garrita!" Celestia said, accepting the hug happily.

A few of the other servants rushed to get their children.

"You guys are alright!" Garrita said, "I was so worried something had happened to you! Why were you gone for so long? You were supposed to lead our people. The war is over."

"We know the war is over," Bridgot said, "We ended it by fulfilling the prophecy. We shall know peace for the next hundred years because of it. It was a longer quest than we thought, but in the end, we were victorious."

"Mommy! Daddy!" came their children's squeals of joy and excitement as they were brought into the throne room.

"Nastazya! Aurano!" Celestia shouted, rushing toward them. Her children ran forward to meet her, and she wrapped them in her arms, happy to see her little ones after so long away. Aurano's blonde curls were bowing over the sides of his head, as he desperately needed a haircut, and Nastazya's wispy brown locks covered Celestia's face as she embraced them, "You guys have gotten so big! I barely recognized you!"

"What happened, mommy?" Nastazya asked.

"Daddy and I stopped the war," Celestia said, "Everything will be alright now. I promise. I'm so happy you guys are safe." She paused, looking at their smiling faces, "Look at those big, beautiful eyes." She cupped their faces in her hands, looking them over. They didn't even have a scratch on them. She smiled, hugging them again.

"Daddy!" They yelled, running to Bridgot.

He had walked to their side as Celestia had been embracing them. Now, it was his turn, as he wrapped his arms around them, hugging them tight.

While Bridgot was reuniting with the kids, Celestia turned back to Garrita, "Where's my mother? Did you find her?"

Garrita looked down, nodding.

"Where is she? Take me to her."

Celestia followed Garrita from the throne room, leaving the kids with Bridgot. She led her down the hall to one of the guest rooms. When they reached the door, Garrita knocked. A doctor answered, looking at them. On seeing Celestia, he allowed them inside.

A knot formed in her stomach that the door had been answered by a doctor. When she entered, she saw her mother lying on the bed, looking weak and sickly. She was covered in sweat; all color drained from her face. She was unconscious, and Celestia turned to the doctor, "What's wrong with her?"

"She sustained a great many injuries," he said, "She's lost a lot of blood."

"She was missing for a few days," Garrita interjected, "We were all searching for her. Some of the other servants found her. She was in the woods, limping along. She had been trying to get back here from the safe-house."

"She must not have had any choice," Celestia said, "She couldn't have known the war was over. Coming back here might have meant her death."

"I don't think she knew where any of us lived," Garrita said, "It was only by chance that Natasha and the kids found us. We saw them running through town, and brought them in. If Lady Eva was still at the safe-house, alone and injured, she would not have been able to make it to town, even if she knew to find us there."

"Whatever the case," the doctor said, "It was lucky we found her when we did. She may not have survived another day."

"Then, you can save her?" Celestia asked.

The doctor gave her a look, and she knew exactly what it meant. She went to her mother's bedside, removing the blanket over her. The sight before her horrified her, and she was almost willing to jeopardize the peace to track down the soldiers who'd done this. Her mother was sliced torso to feet, with many gashes. They had obviously been made by swords.

"They must've thought they'd killed her," she whispered. Thinking of how her untrained mother must've tried to fight them with a sword, only to get cut up and left for dead infuriated her. She could feel her powers fizzling through her, ready to burst forth.

Garrita nearly fainted at the sight, and the doctor made her leave the room.

Celestia allowed her powers to explode from her, and the doctor also fled the room, out of fear. She placed her hand over the first cut, saying, "*Shuleas.*" She went along each and every cut, slowly draining her energy from so much healing. When she was done, she could see that the cuts were healed, but her mother still was not well. She called for another doctor, and one was brought forth immediately. She released her powers so as not to scare the next one.

He came in and checked her mother over, "She needs nourishment. Food and drink are the best things for her condition. But, she would need to wake in order to consume anything. I'm afraid there's nothing I can do for her."

"Thank you, doctor," she said, excusing him. When they were alone again, she allowed her powers to once more course through her veins. She placed her hand over her mother's heart and allowed emotion to take control, not knowing a spell that would help.

Suddenly, her mother woke, sucking in a large breath, and looking around in a panic.

"Food and drink!" Celestia yelled, "Bring food and drink, right now!"

Within seconds, there were servants inside bringing meat, vegetables, and water. Celestia made sure her mother ate and drank plenty before allowing her to relax. She didn't want her to sleep yet, however, as she wanted to ensure the food and drink made it through her first.

"Mother," she said when the servants were gone, "It's me."

"I know," Lady Eva said, "I knew you'd make it back."

"No, you didn't," Celestia retorted.

"No," she said, "I didn't."

"We did it, mom," she told her, "We did it."

Eva smiled, "That's good news, dear. I knew you could do it."

Celestia let out a laugh, "No, you didn't."

"That one was true," she replied, "I believed in you. I still do."

"What happened to you?" she asked.

Eva sighed, "I tried to hold off the soldiers. I tried to be you." She gave her daughter a weak smile, touching her hand, "I've always admired you, for your skill, your bravery, your independence. I just wanted to keep the kids safe. At least I managed that. But, I just couldn't do what you can do."

"You're not trained, mother," she said, "I've had sword training. It's not that you're not as strong or brave; it's that you haven't been taught how. You did the best you could. You saved my children's lives, and the lives of Kgansten's family. I'm proud to call you my mother."

She smiled again, "And I'm proud to call you my daughter."

Bridgot came through the door then, bringing Aurano and Nastazya with him.

"Go see grandma," he said, "But, be careful."

The two children crossed the room, standing beside their mother. Celestia lifted them onto the bed beside their grandma, allowing them to give her hugs.

"Oh, my two beautiful grandkids," she said, "I'm so glad all of you are safe."

"Alright," Celestia said, "Time to let grandma rest." She lifted her kids down from the bed and sent them with her husband.

"Come on, you two," Bridgot said, "Time for bed. Let's go get our pajamas on and get tucked in."

"Okay, daddy!" Nastazya shouted, skipping off down the hall.

Aurano groaned, dragging his feet as he followed his father out of the room.

"They grow up so fast," Eva said.

"Yes, they do," Celestia agreed, "Too fast."

"Make sure you enjoy all the little moments along the way," she said, "not like I did."

"You did the best you could," she said, "I love you, mom."

"I love you, too," she replied, "Now, you go get some rest. I can see that you're tired. Don't worry about me. I'll be fine. You've done enough. I need rest, too, if I am to heal."

She nodded, "Okay, mom. Here," she handed her a bell, "ring this if you need anything."

"I will, dear," she said, "Go on."

Celestia reluctantly left the room, going to say *goodnight* to her children before going to bed herself. Seeing Aurano and Nastazya tucked into bed like any normal night made her smile. She knew everything was going back to normal, and that they would be alright. They were all going to make it through this, as they had made it through everything else that had come their way.

"Goodnight, my angel," Celestia said, kissing Aurano's forehead, and watching his blue eyes crinkle up when her lips touched his head.

She left her son's room, closing the door behind her, and heading into her daughter's room.

"Goodnight, sweetie," she said to Nastazya, kissing her forehead as well. Her daughter's gray eyes twinkled like her father's, and she smiled. Her children were safe, her home was restored, and her family was whole again. As she left her daughter's room that night, she couldn't help but feel light. The weight of the world was no longer on her shoulders. She was free.

Queen Celestia paced nervously back and forth, her flowing blue gown trailing behind her. "I don't know, Garrita," she said, "What if none of our old allies show?"

Celestia was a pale beauty, with long, white-blonde hair and blue eyes. Upon her head sat a silver tiara, and upon her face, a worried expression.

"Well, of course, they'll show, milady," Garrita said. She was the lady-in-waiting to the queen, close in age, with brown hair and brown eyes. She sighed, "They're your friends. Even though you went through some tough times, I'm sure they've forgiven you."

The queen nodded uncertainly.

"Come on," Garrita said, "We must get you to the party."

The two of them headed down the stone corridor of the castle, and to the huge throne room where the party was to be held. It was full of people already, and she noticed elves, dwarves, and humans alike were present. She was relieved yet nervous to see King Boreas himself was there.

"There you are," King Bridgot said, meeting up with his wife. He wore blue royal robes and a silver crown. A cape fell around his shoulders. He had tan skin, curly brown hair, a brown beard—trimmed short—and soft, gray eyes.

She had always loved those eyes. She smiled, "I was nervous for today, but I see we have a great turn-out."

"They're all here for our daughter," he said, returning her smile.

They headed over to their thrones to await the announcement of their little girl.

It wasn't long before the announcer said, "Presenting the birthday girl, Princess Nastazya of Ivétoiless!"

Everyone applauded as the young princess made her grand entrance. She had pale skin, wispy brown hair, and gray eyes. She wore a little gold dress, with a tiny tiara pinned atop her head. As she made her way to the thrones, King Bridgot and Queen Celestia strode forward to meet her.

"Nastazya," Celestia said, scooping her up, "I can't believe you're five years old today."

Her daughter hugged her, her teddy bear hitting her back as she did.

"Mom," Prince Aurano said from beside them. He had curly, blonde hair and blue eyes. He wore blue royal robes and a small, silver crown upon his head, "Can I go play now?"

"Of course you can, sweetheart," she said, smiling.

"Yes!" he yelled, running off with his friends.

"Me, too?" Princess Nastazya asked.

She smiled again, setting her back down, "Go on." She waved a few servants to keep an eye on them as her daughter darted away, waving her bear in the air, and tackling Kganley, Kganzar, and Nedebarth.

"Queen Celestia," King Boreas said, walking up. He was the tall, dark king of the elves, with pointed ears and angled features. His robes were iridescent, picking up shades of blue and white and purple. She looked at him nervously, unsure what he would say or do.

King Bridgot put his arm around her, and she could feel he, too, was unsure.

"My daughter tells me you fulfilled the prophecy," he said.

"Yes," Celestia answered, "We did, with her help."

King Boreas looked at them, "I failed you. All of you. If it were up to me, our world would be a world of darkness now. I am ashamed of myself, for my actions. I was acting out of fear. I was afraid of losing another elven warrior, especially my own daughter. But, I was wrong. I don't expect you to forgive me. I just wanted you to know."

Celestia paused, looking at her husband, and back at King Boreas, "We forgive you. The elves have long been our friends and allies, and it would be a shame to lose that now."

"Thank you," he said, bowing, "Your words humble me."

She smiled, "Please, enjoy the party. You are an honored guest."

He turned to walk away, and when he did, they could see that Xharia was behind him. She was the daughter of the elf king, with long black hair, intense hazel eyes, and mossy-colored robes.

"Xharia!" Celestia said, hugging her.

Bridgot took his turn as well, smiling, "Good to see you."

"It's good to see the two of you as well," she said.

"What happened with you?" Celestia asked.

"Well, when we reached the dwarven tunnels, the soldiers stared at us in awe and disbelief. They dared not mess with us, and they all left the tunnels in shame. The dwarven warriors took back their kingdoms. When we got to Dirthix, Kgansten had Felix and Seamus escort me out of the tunnels, as he went to face King Thanghor. I journeyed through the land of the elves to my kingdom of Garellis alone. When I arrived, they were all so happy to see me, my mother and sisters rushed out to greet me. I went before my father and presented Aurano's bow and arrow. He took it, and handed it to Thaddeus to return to the Museum of Elven Weapons. Instead of focusing on the quest or the weapon or punishments, he hugged me. He was just so happy I was alive and well, nothing else mattered," Xharia said, looking over at her father.

Celestia smiled, "I'm so glad everything went well. I was worried for you."

"No need to worry," she said, "I became an official elven warrior, and my father decided to finally start allowing us to be seen. He's letting me fight, and letting me travel. My younger sister is traveling as well, with several guards, for scholastic research. My older sister and my mother are thrilled to be able to host parties for neighboring elven kingdoms they never got to meet before. Everything is so different now, and it's all thanks to you."

"No," Bridgot said, "It's thanks to you. We never could have completed the quest without you. If you hadn't gone against your father to help us, we would've had no elven warrior, and we would not have been able to destroy Nazirdok's powers."

Xharia smiled, looking behind them, "I hope we continue to see each other."

"So do we," Bridgot said.

With that, Xharia walked back over to the other elves who had come. Bridgot and Celestia turned to see Kgansten and his family nearby, waiting. Kgansten was a red-bearded Dwarf Lord. His wife, Natasha, had silky, black hair and violet eyes. Their three curly red-haired boys were off playing with Princess Nastazya.

Bridgot and Celestia each hugged Kgansten, happy to see their dear friend.

"You made it," Celestia said.

"Good to see you," Bridgot said.

"What happened with your uncle?" Celestia asked.

"When I got to Dirthix, I sent Xharia on, so she could return to her people, and not get caught up in *my* mission," Kgansten said, "I went before my uncle, presenting the axe of Kgoresh the Terrible, to be returned to the Dwarven Hall of Weapons, where it belongs. When I confronted him about what he'd done, he apologized. He admitted he was wrong, and an unfit king, and he gracefully stepped down."

"He stepped down?" Celestia asked in surprise.

Kgansten nodded.

"So, who's the king of the dwarves, now?" Bridgot asked.

"My cousin, Thanghor's son, Thungsten," Kgansten replied.

"Do you think he will make a good king?" Bridgot asked.

"I believe he will," Kgansten answered, "I believe he will." After a pause, he said, "So, what became of the sword of Vidar the Conqueror?"

King Bridgot looked to his wife, smiling, "It is displayed beside the sword of Derekkian, in the Weapons Museum of Ivétoiless."

"Derekkian?" Kgansten asked, "I've never heard of him."

He smiled again, "It's a good story. If you stay awhile after the party, I shall tell it to you. He is the one who defeated Vidar the Conqueror."

"Really?" he asked in amazement, "He should be more famous."

"Yes, he should," Bridgot agreed, looking over at Nastazya's brothers, pleased to see they had made it to the party.

"I see you made it home alright," Celestia said, smiling at Natasha.

"Yes," she answered, "The boys and I had a safe trip back. When we got there, we discovered Thungsten was the new king, and Kgansten was there waiting. We got our home back. We got our lives back." She smiled, giving Kgansten a quick kiss.

"I'm happy for you both," she said.

"What happened with you?" Kgansten asked.

"Yes," Natasha said, "Did you ever find your mother?"

"Sorry I'm late," a familiar voice said from behind them suddenly, "You know I wouldn't miss my granddaughter's birthday for the world!"

"Mom!" Celestia exclaimed, turning and embracing her mother.

"Hello, darling," Eva said, "And hello to you as well, Bridgot." She hugged her son-in-law, smiling. Eva had light brown skin, brown eyes, and caramel hair. She wore a flowing, lavender gown, and a gold band around her head—a symbol of her previous status as queen. She looked amazing, and Celestia was ecstatic to see her health had improved so greatly.

"You look wonderful," Bridgot said.

"Thank you," Eva said, turning to her daughter, "Go greet your guests, darling. I'm quite good at mingling. I'll be here after the party."

Celestia could see that Bridgot's family was there, and even Thaandor had made it. But, the only guest she cared about at that moment was her mother. "I'm just so happy you're well, mother," she said.

"It's all thanks to you," she replied.

"I owed it to you," Celestia said, "for saving my children."

"Nonsense," her mother retorted, "They're my grandchildren. What was I supposed to do? Let them get hurt? Never."

Bridgot smiled, "You did well, Eva."

"So did you," she said, "So did both of you."

"I agree," Kgansten said.

"Me, too," Xharia assented, walking up.

"I second that," Thaandor said, coming over.

"We *all* did well," Celestia said finally, "And, because of that, the prophecy is *finally* fulfilled."

"Looks like we get to enjoy a hundred years of peace," Bridgot said.

Celestia laughed, "Yes. Yes, we do."

THE END

Pronunciation Guide

Characters:

Celestia	(seh-less-tee-uh)
Bridgot	(brī-jut)
Aurano	(or-on-oh)
Kgansten	(gan-sten)
Nastazya	(nuh-stah-zee-uh)
Ezmyra	(ehz-mee-ruh)
Xharia	(zah-ree-uh)
Thaandor	(thann-door)
Nazirdok	(nuh-zeer-dock)
Zandor	(zan-door)
Kyja	(ky-zha)

Cities/Kingdoms/Villages:

Ivétoiless	(eve-ay-twol-ess)
Kataran	(kat-uh-ran)
Garellis	(guh-rell-iss)
Dirthix	(der-thix)
Khanjgi	(con-jee)
Kiteau	(ki-toh)
Chemsson	(shem-son)

Countries/Lands:

Duwazo	(dew-way-zo)
Katangalo	(kat-ann-gall-oh)
Gliken	(glī-ken)
Korga	(core-guh)
Gachichken	(guh-cheech-ken)
Abyumo	(ab-bee-you-moh)
Cardeas	(car-dee-yes)
Fluorasti	(floor-ah-stee)
Mashang	(muh-shang)
Kogatsa	(koh-got-suh)
Kuttub	(kut-tub)
Millhaymae	(mill-hay-may)

Spells

Balgadeer: like Facetime for wizards, allowing them to contact each other through reflective surfaces, or with non-magic beings through a witch's glass

Harrow: knocks opponents back

Depugno: shoots magical arrows through opponents, killing them (can pierce armor)

Shuleas: heals flesh wounds

Cerco: creates a protective barrier, or a "force field" of sorts

Shuleor: heals broken bones

Shulee: heals cuts and bruises

Chulen: cures common cold

Dwervo: produces water

Pheonor: produces fire

Pheonir: produces heat

Sithen: removes poison

Peore: blooms flowers

Goncor: moves objects

Heassaren: steams garments

Sponj: cleans skin

Wacour: cleans hair

Shift: sweeps the floor

Levei: dusts furniture

Carbonis: stores energy in an inanimate object

Momento: teleports the target of the spell from one location to another

Configlie: spell of magical destruction

Vera: makes beings and things warm and dry

Corsen: forms a magical umbrella

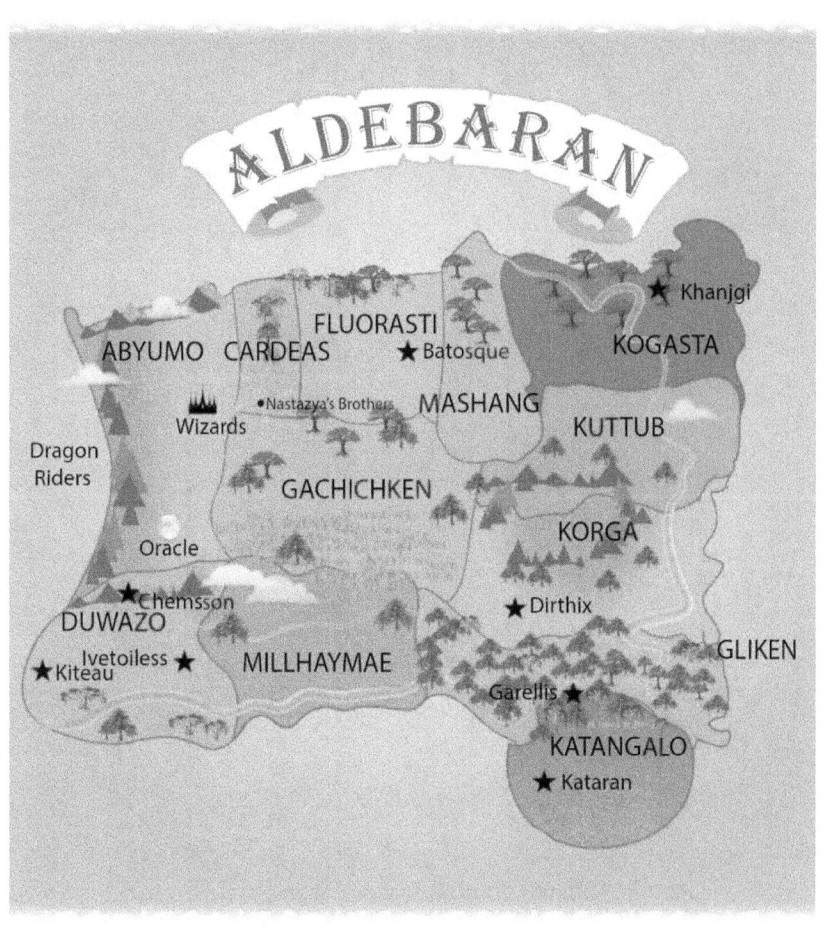

The Star Chronicles

Book 1: *When the Stars Align*

Book 2: *When the Stars Fall*

Book 3: *When the Stars Collide*

www.ingramcontent.com/pod-product-compliance
Lightning Source LLC
Chambersburg PA
CBHW050405030726
47503CB00006B/2036